"You are, hands down, the fastest female in the West."

Landry winced. "Translate that to—takes little time with her appearance."

"Some women's appearances don't need time."

A compliment? From Chase? Her eyes widened.

Various birds chirped and sang as they strolled the thirty yards to the river in a comfortable silence. Once they reached the bank, they set their gear down and went to work baiting their hooks.

Landry chose a fat worm, slid it onto her hook.

"Impressive, Malone. Apparently you have no qualms about an earthworm's death."

"Shh, you'll scare the fish away."

He chuckled, baited his hook, moved up the river from her a bit.

As the distance widened between them, she started breathing easier. Why was Chase giving her contradictory signals?

He didn't even like her. Did he?

Whether *he* liked her or not, *she* liked this new Chase. Maybe too much.

Shannon Taylor Vannatter is a stay-at-home mom/pastor's wife/award-winning author. She lives in a rural central-Arkansas community with a population of around one hundred, if you count a few cows. Contact her at shannonvannatter.com.

Books by Shannon Taylor Vannatter

Love Inspired

Texas Cowboys

Reuniting with the Cowboy
Winning Over the Cowboy

Love Inspired Heartsong Presents

Rodeo Ashes
Rodeo Regrets
Rodeo Queen
Rodeo Song
Rodeo Family
Rodeo Reunion

Visit the Author Profile page
at Harlequin.com for more titles.

Winning Over the Cowboy

Shannon Taylor Vannatter

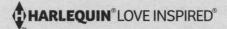

Recycling programs
for this product may
not exist in your area.

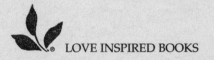

LOVE INSPIRED BOOKS

ISBN-13: 978-0-373-89923-4

Winning Over the Cowboy

Copyright © 2017 by Shannon Taylor Vannatter

All rights reserved. Except for use in any review, the reproduction or utilization of this work in whole or in part in any form by any electronic, mechanical or other means, now known or hereinafter invented, including xerography, photocopying and recording, or in any information storage or retrieval system, is forbidden without the written permission of the editorial office, Love Inspired Books, 195 Broadway, New York, NY 10007 U.S.A.

This is a work of fiction. Names, characters, places and incidents are either the product of the author's imagination or are used fictitiously, and any resemblance to actual persons, living or dead, business establishments, events or locales is entirely coincidental.

This edition published by arrangement with Love Inspired Books.

® and TM are trademarks of Love Inspired Books, used under license. Trademarks indicated with ® are registered in the United States Patent and Trademark Office, the Canadian Intellectual Property Office and in other countries.

www.Harlequin.com

Printed in U.S.A.

It is better to trust in the LORD
than to put confidence in man.
—*Psalms* 118:8

To Texas Mom, who always makes visiting her in Texas Hill Country feel like coming home.

Chapter One

Her best friend wasn't here anymore. And never would be again.

A knot clogged in Landry's throat as she stood in the gravel drive. The early evening Texas sky blurred, and she blinked the moisture away.

The massive cedar structure with the endless green metal roof looked exactly as it had when she'd lived and worked here seven years before. The same as when she'd visited last fall. Nothing about the dude ranch had changed. Yet everything had.

"May I help you?" A male voice.

Landry shaded her eyes from the mid-July glare, searched the porch. Eden's brother? Or a ranch hand? Blinded by the sun, she couldn't tell.

Besides, she'd only met the brother three times. Two funerals and a wedding. Sounded like some rom-com, but there was nothing romantic or funny about it.

"I'm Landry Malone." *Here to claim my inheritance.* As she neared the house, her vision cleared. Despite the Stetson shadowing his features, she made out Eden's brother. Green eyes, raven hair. But the similarities ended there. The brother was all male, stubbly beard and stiff posture—a cowboy to the bone.

His gaze narrowed as she stepped up on the porch. "I'm Chase Donovan."

"We met here at—" A rush of memories choked off her words. The backyard draped in tulle. Eden so happy, rushing off in cloud of birdseed. The last time Landry had seen her. Nine months and one week ago. She swallowed hard. "At Granny's— your grandmother's funeral. At Eden's wedding." And again at her funeral.

"I remember." His mouth tightened, but he clasped the hand she offered, stiff and somehow disapproving. Checked his watch, as if she were late.

But she wasn't. She was exactly on time. Was he one of those uptight people who arrived ten to fifteen minutes early wherever he went? Surely not, with his nomad lifestyle.

"We'll talk in the office." Despite his dour welcome, Chase opened the door for her.

A blast of air-conditioning pebbled her heated skin.

"I know where it is." Her stomach sank. Did he plan to sell, without even talking it over? He couldn't. Eden loved this place. Lived and breathed it. And it was their family's heritage.

Same hardwood floors, log furnishings, cowhide chairs. Homey and safe. She wanted to look around more, but his hurried cowboy boots thudded behind her like he had somewhere else to be. One of his long strides ate up three of hers as she crossed the foyer.

She made it to the office doorway, blocking Chase with her hesitation. A silver-haired man sat at the rustic ash desk, black reading glasses resting on his bulbous nose. Granny used to sit there. And then Eden.

"Ms. Malone." The man stood, clasped her hand and ushered her inside the room. "I'm William Abbott. We've been expecting you. Please, have a seat."

Landry settled in a cowhide chair across the massive desk from him. Chase eased into the one beside her. His long legs sprawled in front of him. Totally at ease.

"As I told you on the phone, the senior Donovans left the Chasing Eden Café to their son, Elliot, and the Chasing Eden Dude Ranch to their grandchildren, Chase and Eden, effectively splitting the business."

It was so much more than a business. It was Granny's legacy. Eden's heritage.

Landry's cell buzzed, and her cheeks heated.

"Need to get that?" Chase drummed his fingers on the desk.

"I forgot to tell my mom I made it here okay."

With a wince, she fished her phone out of her pocket. "Sorry."

"By all means, let her know you're safe." Mr. Abbott's smile was understanding. "I have a daughter."

Afraid to look at Chase, she focused on pulling up the message from Mama. R U there yet?

Yes. Talking to lawyer, she typed as quickly as she could, then turned her phone off. "Sorry."

"As I was saying, upon Eden Donovan Miller's death, her will comes into play," Mr. Abbott continued, unhurried, patient. "Her last wishes were for her husband to take up to a year to decide if he had any interest in running the dude ranch." He scanned the paperwork on the desk.

"Recently, Paxton Miller signed an affidavit that he has no interest in the dude ranch. So according to Eden's will, her half of the business goes to Ms. Landry Malone. The two of you must run the business together for two months. After that, each party may choose to run the business together or appoint another party to run it for ten months."

Run it with Chase? After meeting him, in passing, three times? Now four. Or some stranger he'd appoint? This was her chance. Eden's generosity had given her a reason to escape her hometown. Escape the pitying whispers. Here she'd be owner—or, at least, part owner—of a dude ranch. Instead of the jilted almost-bride. She had to make it work.

Her gaze drifted to the display of family photos on the wall. "And then what?"

"After a year, you each decide whether to keep your holdings or sell."

Surely Chase wouldn't want to sell his family legacy. But she remembered Eden saying he had no interest in running the dude ranch or the restaurant. That he was a free spirit. Instead of attending college, he'd traveled for several years.

"But she's not even family. She can't sell to some outside party." Chase straightened in his chair, tapped the toe of his cowboy boot on the hardwood. "What if Ms. Malone opts out?"

She gasped. Was he already trying to finagle her out of her share? *Why?* He'd only returned from his gallivanting when Granny got sick. And he'd been content working as a trail and fishing guide and handyman while the rest of his family handled the business.

"That's not an option for Ms. Malone. Her only choice is to maintain her share or sell."

"We can't sell." She glanced at Chase, trying to keep her face neutral of the anger that was building. "Not without both of us agreeing. Can we? And how could we even sell the dude ranch when the restaurant is under the same roof?"

"The businesses are separate entities. According to Eden's will, if one party wants to liquidate the dude ranch, the other has first opportunity to buy the selling party out and another six months to acquire the funds for a buyout. The café belongs to Elliot, no matter what's decided about the ranch."

The dude ranch was way out of Landry's league. Her nails dug into the arms of her chair. She could never afford to buy Chase's half on her own. Why had Eden involved her instead of simply leaving it all to her family?

"But we barely know each other," Landry said. "I can't live here with a man I don't even know."

Sarcasm coated Chase's chuckle. "Do you really think Eden would saddle you with me if I were the boogeyman?"

True. Eden had been close to her brother. How many times had she tried to orchestrate a date between Landry and Chase? She would never have tried to fix Landry up with him all those times if he weren't a good man. He was just stiff. And hurting just like she was.

"There's a cabin on the property. I stay there." Chase propped one booted foot on the other knee, drew in a sharp breath. "You can have the private quarters off the communal great room, where Granny lived. My parents' private quarters are still on the other end by the kitchen."

So he'd thought this through. Of course, he'd had more time to get used to the idea than she had. But at least she wouldn't be under the same roof with him. Back when she'd lived here during culinary school, his parents had lived in the cabin.

"Ms. Malone, do you have another party in mind

to manage the property after your two months here?" The lawyer peered at her over his glasses.

"No. I'm staying. If I decide I want to sell, I'll stay until then."

"Very well, then." Mr. Abbott flipped through his calendar. "It's Wednesday, July fifteenth. We'll reconvene on Tuesday, September fifteenth."

Landry had to make this work. And if Chase wanted to sell, she'd figure out a way to get a loan when the time came to buy him out. What other choice did she have? She had to keep Eden's legacy alive. If she didn't, she'd have to go home. Where her entire town felt sorry for her. And she'd have to add *failure* to her *jilted* title.

"Thanks for coming today, Mr. Abbott." Chase stood, shook the lawyer's hand and escorted him to the exit.

A temporary roadblock. That was all Landry Malone could be. He needed to unload her. The sooner she sold, the sooner he could get on with his life. Figure out how to enjoy running the ranch without Eden.

His chest ached. Oh, how he missed her.

Landry Malone had no right to his heritage. Why hadn't Eden willed the dude ranch within the family? They didn't need any outsiders. How had this Malone woman charmed Eden into leaving her half of the dude ranch his grandparents had built from scratch?

Countless times, Eden had tried to get him to come home during his traveling years. To meet her friend. Had the fix-up been Landry's idea, trying to get her talons into him, for the dude ranch? Was she some kind of player? Con artist?

The front door closed behind the lawyer.

"Are your parents here?" Heels clicked across the foyer behind him.

He checked his watch. "By now they're gone to evening Bible study. It's their turn on the rotation schedule." His grandparents had set up the system years ago, always ensuring every staff member had the opportunity to attend church at least once every week.

"I remember." Wistfulness filled her tone. She cleared her throat. "Do you ever talk to Paxton?"

Why was that any of her concern?

"I mean—I know it's none of my business." She lifted one shoulder. "But I'm just curious why he's not interested in Eden's inheritance."

"He moved back to Lubbock, where his family is." His sigh came up from the toes of his boots. "We try to keep in touch. But it's stiff. It's like talking to each other brings back Eden's death. Mom and Dad, too. We love Paxton, but it's hard. For all of us." An understatement.

And why was he telling her this, anyway?

Because it weighed heavy on him. "It's like the piece of the puzzle that connected our lives is missing."

"Have you talked to him about this decision? I mean—if you don't mind me asking?"

"Paxton doesn't feel like he has any claim to the ranch. That it should return to Eden's family. He thought by opting out, it would revert to me. Or Mom and Dad."

"Oh. And then my name popped up." Her tone sounded apologetic.

If she was a scammer, would she be concerned about Paxton? Or maybe her compassion was part of her act.

"Well, I guess I'm it, then." She blew out a big breath. "The first thing we need to do is get this place running smoothly. What about staff? Are the Fletchers still here?"

It was already running smoothly. "Yes. They helped me manage the place during the legal stuff." Until Paxton had come to a decision to forfeit his share and unintentionally saddled Chase with Landry.

"We need to look at the books, the schedule, and figure out what needs to be done. Do you know anything about running a dude ranch?"

"I know my way around." The nerve of her. Maybe she was so uptight because she was roasting in that pin-striped business suit. "I grew up here." *Where were you? Out scamming?* "I've worked here the last three years. I've overseen operations since Eden's…wedding."

Color drained from her face, effectively brightening her strawberry blond waves. "So, you...you were here last fall?"

He knew what she was referring to. Eden had gone to be in Landry's wedding, but for some reason the nuptials hadn't happened. His sister had returned early with Landry in tow and invited her to stay—for free—after the busted romance.

"I was." For almost two weeks, she'd stayed holed up in her room, only coming out for Eden's wedding, then leaving immediately afterward.

Her cheeks flushed. She knew that he knew. Her dark chocolate gaze darted away.

"I worked here for a year and a half when Granny was still alive, while I attended culinary school." She headed back to the office. "Then as a chef at a dude ranch in Aubrey since then. So I can handle the scheduling and cleaning and help with cooking duties if needed. Let's check the schedule."

"I know the schedule." He tailed her. Who did she think she was? Some interloper trying to take over? Not on his watch. This whole thing was surreal. "Nu nu, nu nu, nu nu, nu nu."

"*The Twilight Zone* theme?" She turned to face him. One eyebrow quirked.

"I kind of feel like I passed through the portal."

She snorted. "I love that show." She turned pink, seemingly from embarrassment, then schooled her features back into all business. "Do we have guests booked?"

"We're at the halfway mark of summer break. With school starting up in five weeks, we're about to be inundated with families grabbing their last opportunity at fleeing their ordinary existence."

He'd spend the rest of the day going over the schedule with her, introducing her to staff, familiarizing her with the workings of the dude ranch, the kitchen, especially the cleaning closet. Then he'd hit her with memorizing their rates and accommodations. Maybe she'd run screaming from the place.

But he doubted it. Something told him it wouldn't be easy to get rid of Landry Malone. Yet he'd find a way. And the fact that she appreciated his favorite vintage television show wouldn't sway him.

Chase had followed Landry around for the rest of the day, stiff and unfriendly. Nothing like Eden. Nothing like their parents. Nothing like Granny. Would his parents be glad to see her?

Or would they resent her, too? She held her breath as Chase opened the kitchen door for her.

His parents' sported disposable bouffant food prep caps, their heads bent over the counter.

Janice looked up from kneading dough, her apron dusted with flour. "Landry." She wiped her hands on her apron, scurried over and greeted her with a hug. "How nice to have you here."

Elliot's smile awakened the laugh lines at the

corners of his eyes. "It'll be a relief to have another chef to share kitchen duty with."

"Oh, dear." Janice patted at the flour her hug had deposited on Landry's lapel and only made it worse.

"It's okay. It's washable." For the first time since her arrival, she felt welcome. "I'm so glad to see y'all." Her vision blurred with the sudden longing to cry with relief.

"It's almost nine o'clock." Janice went back to her dough. "When did you get here?"

"About five." Chase answered for her. "Y'all were gone to evening Bible study by the time we finished with William."

Landry stifled a yawn. "Chase has been showing me around, getting me familiar with operations."

"You must be exhausted." Janice frowned. "Get her settled in, son."

"But shouldn't we go over the kitchen schedule?" Chase settled on a stool at the breakfast bar, his long legs still reaching the floor.

"We'll talk about it in the morning."

"Yes, ma'am." Chase stood.

"Sleep in tomorrow." Elliot gave her a wink.

"Don't mind Chase." Janice turned the dough. "He never runs out of steam."

"Have a good night." At least his parents were on her side.

Chase ushered Landry out, handed her a key. "I

had Ron put your things in Granny's room. You know where it is." He headed for the front door, exited.

Leaving her standing there, uncertain, clearly unwanted. Did he treat all guests like this? Probably just her. Because she didn't belong.

Becca and Ron descended the stairs, laughing together. The Fletchers hadn't changed. Becca with her long brown hair, painfully thin frame and kind blue eyes. Ron was still thick and stocky—the same height as his wife, ruddy complexion and thunderous voice.

"Landry!" he boomed.

"Oh, I'm so glad you're back." Becca clasped both her hands.

"Thanks."

"We were just leaving. But since you're here—"

"Y'all go. I was headed to my quarters myself. We'll catch up tomorrow."

"See you then." Becca gave her a quick hug, then linked fingers with her husband and exited.

Two more allies. With Chase's chill toward her and quiet wariness from the rest of the employees—food preps, waitstaff, cleaning personnel, ranch hands—she felt like a definite outsider. They probably saw her as an intruder just like Chase did. Possibly worried about their jobs with so much change.

Landry crossed the foyer, cut through the great

room and unlocked the door to Granny's private quarters.

The entire dude ranch was constructed with exposed massive beams, rock work and wood everywhere. Log furnishings, nail heads, leather, cowhide and deer antler chandeliers. But Granny's quarters had drywall and were filled with Victorian rose fabrics, lace and white wicker. A sanctuary.

Landry perched on the end of the bed and closed her eyes. After all the guests were settled, she and Eden used to spend hours in this room. Still in college, they'd shared their hopes and dreams with Granny, giggled over guys, tried on new makeup and hair tips. Had it really been seven years ago? Seemed like yesterday. It was here that Landry's dream was born. To own a dude ranch someday.

Last fall when she'd visited, Granny had been gone. Eden had lived in these quarters then and had tried to put Landry back together after Kyle had dumped her. All in the midst of getting ready for her own wedding.

Landry had never imagined it would be the last time she'd see her best friend. Never imagined she'd end up as part owner here. Without Granny. Without Eden. But with Chase.

A chorus of crickets, owls and frogs echoed outside. It was too quiet in this huge house. Even with Janice and Elliot, a few of the staff and several guests, Landry felt alone.

But tomorrow they'd be hopping, according to the schedule. Staying busy would keep her mind off missing Eden. Missing Granny. Missing what her life was supposed to be.

She strolled to the window. The light from Chase's cabin glowed in the distance. Such a peaceful night. But she'd never sleep.

Maybe fresh air would clear her mind. Stop it from spinning. She crossed the great room and the foyer, then stepped out.

Into a solid wall. "Oomph."

"Whoa." Chase's strong hands on her shoulders steadied her. "Watch where you're going."

A nervous giggle tangled in her throat. "I would if I could. But I can't see a thing."

"Ever heard of a flashlight?"

"I thought you left for your cabin. What are you doing lurking on the front porch?"

"I own this front porch. Half of it, anyway." The challenge echoed in his tone. "I was just trying to relax in the swing, heard somebody moving about, thought it was Mom and Dad."

"Oh." She hugged herself. "I just needed some air."

"I'll leave you to it, then." The porch creaked with his heavy footfalls as he strode away from her. She heard the crunch of gravel and after that... silence.

Slowly her eyes adjusted to the darkness, and she made her way to the porch swing, settling in the already warm middle part of the cushion. So he'd told the truth. He hadn't been lurking. Yet she got the distinct impression Chase Donovan didn't trust her.

But he needed her. And tomorrow, she'd just have to show him how indispensable she truly was.

Chase stopped on the porch and steeled himself, then opened the door to the ranch house.

Landry greeted him from the check-in counter with a bright smile, framed by the huge metal Lone Star on the wall behind her.

He'd half expected her to sleep in her first morning here. But here she was. She'd fastened her hair up into a high ponytail with the sides swooped low, covering her ears.

"Morning." He tipped his hat.

"Good morning. What's on the agenda today? I mean—other than three families arriving with numerous kids in tow."

So she'd studied the reservations for the day. "There's a drip under the sink in the Rest a Spell Room—and the toilet flushes slow in the Trail Boss Room. Don't guess you know anything about plumbing."

"I know a coupling from an elbow."

"Really?" His voice and eyebrows kicked up a notch. "Want to be my plumber's helper?"

"Sure." She scurried out from behind the counter as if this was the highlight of her day. Wearing jeans, a casual purple blouse, tennis shoes. At least she was dressed more appropriately for work on a ranch than she had been yesterday.

Was she trying to impress him? Win him over? *Don't hold your breath, sweetheart.*

He strolled through the office to the maintenance closet, grabbed his plumbing box, turned and almost crashed into her.

"Oh, sorry." She reached for the box. "Need anything else out of there? I can carry something."

So eager to please. "I've got it."

She turned away, crossed the office and headed for the stairs.

"It's the third room on the—"

"I remember."

He followed her up the stairs in silence, their footfalls echoing. He hadn't figured out just how yet, but someway, he'd send Landry Malone screaming all the way back to Aubrey, Texas. By the end of the week. If not sooner.

At the top, she headed straight to the Rest a Spell Room, unlocked the door, held it open for him.

"This room was always one of my favorites." She spun a circle in the middle of the space, scanning the barn wood walls and ceiling, then ran her hand over the suede bedspread. "So soothing. Lives up to its name. I stayed here when Ky— I stayed here last fall."

When Ky what?

He slid the barn door open, strolled into the

bathroom, set his toolbox down, opened the cabinet under the sink and knelt in front of it with a flashlight.

"Looks like a simple coupling on the cold." He ran his finger along the dripping pipe.

"Do I need to turn the water off?"

"I can do that here." He turned, eased onto his back, leaning on his elbows, and stretched his legs out in the cramped space. "Can you hand me that hacksaw and find the smallest coupling?"

"You mean the half-inch?" She settled on the floor cross-legged with her knee almost touching his, dug the hacksaw out of the plastic toolbox and handed it to him.

"You know your stuff." In the three times they'd met, she'd been mostly quiet, maybe even uncomfortable. Because of Eden's attempts at a fixup?

Despite his determination to resent her, she kept impressing him. Add to that, she was easy on the eyes with her unruly strawberry blond waves, enormous brown eyes a man could drown in and a smattering of freckles across her perky nose.

"My parents own a Christian bookstore with a coffee bar. I've helped my dad with lots of plumbing over the years."

"So you're a Christian?"

Silence. Maybe not.

"I am. But I've had a lot going on. Haven't been to church in a while." Her gaze dropped to the floor, then bounced back up to his. "You?"

"He got me through Eden's death."

"Me, too."

Maybe they did have something in common. Other than Eden. But he couldn't let his guard down with her. He lay back and stuck his head under the counter, banging his elbow in the process.

Heat shot through the length of his arm. "Ouch. That was my funny bone, and I didn't find it humorous at all." He clutched his right elbow.

"Sorry." Sympathy edged her voice.

He reached for the coupling, and her fingers grazed his. "Do we have any disinfectant mold killer?"

"I think I saw some."

He slid the hacksaw into the tight space, drew the teeth carefully across the pipe. There was a trickle of water. Then a burst of it spewed everywhere.

Landry screamed as he fumbled with the shut-off valve got the spray of water back to a trickle, then nothing. He wiped his face and slid out from under the cabinet.

"You did that on purpose." She sat in a tight ball with her back to him. In a puddle, hands covering her head, drenched from head to toe.

"I didn't." But he could barely keep the laughter at bay. "We got to talking and I forgot to turn the valve off. Here. Let me help you." On his knees, he offered his hand.

Her head popped up, drenched tendrils framed her dripping face. She gave him a steely glare, ignoring his offer. But when she tried to get her feet under her, she slid in the puddle.

"Let me help you."

Another glare, but she clutched his hand. She slipped again, tugging him off balance. They both ended up in the puddle side by side, on their backs and soaking wet. He couldn't keep from laughing any longer.

"I know you did that on purpose." She clambered to her knees. "You want to get rid of me. To get me out of your way."

Uh-oh. She was on to him. "I honestly didn't mean to spray you with water. But you're right, I can't say that I really want you around and I don't understand why Eden left you half of *my* legacy."

She propped her hands on her hips. "I'm not going anywhere. For whatever reason, Eden wanted me here."

Had that really been his sister's wish? Or had Landry scammed her into thinking she did? He rolled over, managed to stand.

"I didn't do it on purpose. I promise." But maybe he should have. If he made her miserable enough, maybe she'd leave. If she left, surely he and his parents could manage to buy her out.

"Let me help you up." He offered his hand.

Her gaze bored into his. But with little choice, she laid her hand in his.

Just outside the puddle, he braced his feet and helped her up.

Her feet slid, but he steadied her with his hands on her waist.

Standing in the middle of the puddle, eyes intense, she pressed her face close to his. "I. Loved. Her. Too." Her words came through clenched teeth, as a tear slid down her cheek.

His gut turned over. If she was an actress, she was a good one. Good enough to take Hollywood by storm. Could she be for real?

There was a knock on the door, and it quickly swung open as Becca stepped in and spied them in the bathroom. "Oh. I'm on cleaning rounds."

"We had a little mishap." His arms dropped to his sides, then clasped Landry's fingers in his. "Careful. Don't slip, now."

She tiptoed out of the puddle, then jerked her hand out of his grasp.

Becca's wide eyes took in all of it, pinging from one to the other.

"Don't worry about this mess. I'll handle it." He stepped around the pooling water, grabbed a towel and then mopped up the worst of it.

"Yes, sir." Becca exited.

Landry shivered, then hugged herself. "Thanks to you, I must look like a drowned rat." She spun on her heel and stalked out of the room.

A pretty drowned rat. A dangerous one.

Yet her intensity when she'd claimed to love

Eden, too, tugged at him. But he couldn't just blindly trust a stranger with half of his inheritance at stake.

As soon as he got a minute, he'd Google her. He should have done it when William first told him about her being in Eden's will. But he'd been too busy keeping the dude ranch running.

It was time to check this woman out. If Landry Malone had skeletons in her closet, he'd find them.

Chapter Two

Birdsong heralded the bright summer morning. But Chase was all keyed up, despite the peace that always hovered over his grandfather's old fishing cabin. Three axis deer, two whitetail and dozens of fish looked on from the pine walls. His grandfather's hunting successes captured for eternity through the art of taxidermy. They always made Chase feel close to Gramps.

After her dousing, Chase hadn't seen any more of Landry yesterday. Probably holed up in her quarters, licking her wounds. He could only hope she was packing.

His stomach knotted in anticipation as he set his coffee mug by his computer and typed in her name.

The search quickly produced an engagement announcement. He clicked on the newspaper and saw a professional-looking color photo. Landry was all smiles, standing behind a preppy blond man, her arms wrapped around his shoulders.

Mr. and Mrs. Kyle Reginald Billings Sr. announce the engagement of their son, Kyle

Reginald Billings Jr., to Ms. Landry Ann Malone.

Mr. Billings Jr. is the chief operating officer of his family-owned corporation, Data Solutions, based in Dallas. Ms. Malone is a chef at Warren Dude Ranch in Aubrey. Mr. and Mrs. Billings Jr. will reside at their newly purchased Arbor Bed-and-Breakfast in Denton.

Chase checked the date. Almost a year ago, early September. Only weeks before she came to stay at the dude ranch. Why hadn't the wedding happened?

Mr. Billings Jr. was obviously loaded. Had Landry landed him for his money? Was that why the wedding didn't happen? He'd figured her out and called it off? She apparently hadn't ended up with the B and B or she wouldn't have come here.

Chase backed out of the newspaper link, then clicked on her Facebook page. It took him a few tries to remember the password his sister had used when she set up the dude ranch's account, but finally he was in, and Landry's wall soon popped up.

My happily-ever-after is only 1 hour away. With a dozen smiley faces.

It was her last post—on what should have been her wedding day. Nothing since. He scrolled down.

My happily-ever-after is only 1 day away.

He continued to scroll. She'd counted the days from the time of her engagement to her wedding day. Three months—every day interspersed with photos of traditional wedding dresses, flowers, cakes and decorations. Amidst it all, an elegant ultramodern dress completely different than the others with the comment, My dress Kyle chose.

Countless pictures of simple bouquets of those purple, droopy flowers that grew on vines in trees. An elaborate bouquet: My flowers Kyle chose.

Dozens of unpretentious two-and three-layer cakes with a bride and groom on top. A fussy cake with a roses spiraled up and around six layers, topped by a bride and groom in a glittery carriage: My wedding cake Kyle chose.

Looked like Kyle hijacked the wedding. Had Landry bailed because he was too controlling?

Three months worth of days focused solely on her wedding. Nothing else. Nothing about what she'd had for dinner, or vacation pictures, or "my cat did this or that" posts. Like a giddy bride and not a gold digger.

Pressure mounted in his chest as he clicked on her photos. He'd never been such a snoop.

No photos of her fiancé. Or of them together, for that matter. The only other pictures were of rustic dude ranches. With one fancy B and B in the mix. The caption: The Arbor Bed-and-Breakfast Kyle bought.

He closed the browser, guilt churning his gut.

He was basically stalking her online. But with good reason. He had to figure her out. If she was a scam artist, he needed to know. He'd had his fill of those.

But did scam artists count down the days to their happily-ever-afters? Maybe if they were trying to reel in a rich guy. And right after her wedding-that-wasn't, she'd landed at the dude ranch. In the Rest a Spell Room.

What had she said yesterday—she'd stayed there after Ky? Kyle. After Kyle what? His sister had been tight-lipped about the circumstances. Had Landry set a plan in motion to console herself with Chase's family legacy?

He downed the rest of his coffee, grabbed his keys and locked up. Gravel crunched under his boots as he made his way to the ranch house.

If he was honest with himself, he knew Landry couldn't have foreseen Eden's diving accident or that she'd be named a beneficiary. And Landry seemed genuine. He could usually get a good read on people. Wasn't easy to pull one over on him. He'd just have to spend time with her—figure her out a piece at a time. Until the puzzle that made up Landry Malone was complete.

Might as well get to it.

Day three. What would Chase pull today in his quest to get rid of her? Maybe they could forget yesterday and start over. She drew in a deep breath and crossed the great room, ready for battle.

He sat in a wingback in the foyer, reading a horse magazine. Her steps stalled.

Seemed harmless. But she'd keep an eye on him. Just in case.

The phone rang.

"You can get it." He didn't move.

Of course she could. She was half owner and didn't need his permission.

She hurried to the reservation desk, grabbed the handset. "Chasing Eden Dude Ranch. May I help you?"

"Yes." A pleasant-sounding woman. "I'd like to book a room for a week. We'd arrive a week from today. Do you have anything available?"

"Let me check." She scanned the calendar on the screen. "How many people?"

"Two adults, two children."

With Chase's scrutiny, it took all her concentration to do a mental inventory of their rooms that would suit the caller's needs.

"We have the Roundup Room, which has a queen and a twin bunk bed. Or we have the Tarry Awhile Room with a king-size bed. That room connects to our Wild Horses Room with two twin beds." She quoted rates on both setups. "We also have an all inclusive package with trail rides, fishing trips, camping and three meals a day." She quoted more rates. "Or you can pay only for the activities you utilize and meals when you dine in."

"We're visiting family near, so we'll probably spend most of our days and meals with them. The two rooms sound perfect, though. Can we get both of them for the whole week?"

"You can." Landry settled at the desk. "Let's confirm dates, and then I'll need a name for the reservation and a credit card."

As she entered all the information in the desktop, she glanced at Chase. Watching her.

She closed her eyes, forced her focus back to the caller. "Since you have family near, have you been to our area before, Mrs. Collins?"

"Yes."

"We usually offer to mail a brochure of area attractions in advance." To encourage potential guests not to change their minds, Chase had instructed. "Would you be interested in that?"

"We'll just pick one up when we get there."

"All right, then." She scanned the screen, making sure she'd entered everything required. "I have all that I need. We'll look forward to your stay, Mrs. Collins. If you have any questions or concerns in the meantime, please don't hesitate to call."

"Thank you so much."

She ended the call. Without missing a beat, it rang again.

"Go for it." He flipped a magazine page.

So, did he expect her to play receptionist while he chilled out? "Chasing Eden Dude Ranch. May I help you?"

"Yes." A contrite woman's voice. "I'd like to cancel our reservation for next week, please. The Martin family."

Landry scanned to the reservation on the computer. A family of six—two rooms. "May I reschedule your stay for you?" She copied the reservation, credit info included, ready to paste somewhere else.

"No. I'm sorry, but Horseshoe Trails is running a special. We found a better deal."

"I hate to hear that." Should she offer to match the deal? Not without knowing what it was. Not without discussing it with her partner. Her gaze crashed into Chase's. "Would you like to sign up for our newsletter to keep you informed on when we run specials?"

"That sounds good." The woman carefully enunciated her email address.

Landry read it back to confirm. "Please keep us in mind for your next stay."

The line went dead.

"Another cancellation? Let me guess. They're taking their business to Horseshoe Trails." Chase set his coffee cup down with a thunk.

"How did you know?"

"It's the third one. Kind of cancels out the booking you made earlier. What was that about a newsletter and specials?"

"I think we should start one, and we need to discuss specials." She wrote down the competition's name on a scratchpad, circled it and underlined it. "Where is Horseshoe Trails?"

"Right down the road. Back when Granny and Gramps opened this place, there were only a few other dude ranches in the area. Now there are at least a dozen, and we all fight for guests." He nabbed his coffee, stood and then strolled into the office.

She chased after him, stopped at his side in front of the back window. Miles of woods interspersed with pastures. Peaceful, like coming home.

"This place was always hopping when we were kids," he said. "With trail rides, cattle drives, fishing and camping trips year-round. And the swimming pool in the summer. Never a dull moment, and guests had to book well in advance."

"I know you want it to stay that way. So do I." She hated to ask, but it was her business, too. "Is the ranch losing money?"

"Not yet. But business has been down. In the off-seasons, we barely break even."

"We have to do something." A hummingbird flitted about the feeder until another dive-bombed him.

"What can we do?" He splayed his free hand. "We can't force people to stay here."

"No. But we can find ways to lure them here." The hummingbirds did a jousting dance in the air before the dominant one won. Much like her and Chase. "Do you know what Horseshoe Trails's special is?"

"No."

"We need to find out." She turned to the desk, settled in the chair, Googled Horseshoe Trails. "Fifteen percent off regular room prices. And their all-inclusive package is ten percent cheaper than ours. Through August."

"That's basically giving rooms away." He paced behind her. "We can't pay our staff at those rates."

"Can we pay our staff if we keep losing reservations?"

"Let me guess." He stopped pacing at the back window. "You think we should match the offer?"

"We beat it. Drop our room prices and inclusive package five percent cheaper than theirs. Only for the rest of the summer."

"You think that will work?" He claimed the nail-head chair across from her, sipped his coffee.

"Well, it's not working as-is."

"What about the guests who already have reservations?"

"We'll specify that it starts with reservations made this week." The desk chair made a creaking sound as she leaned back. "It won't apply to already booked guests. Unless they call to cancel. Or unless they mention it."

He hooked his leg over the arm of the chair. "We can give it a try. But what if they beat our offer?"

"We'll cross that bridge if we get there." She lifted one shoulder. "Give me the password for the website and I'll set it up."

He hesitated, gaze locked on hers. "Only members of our family have the password."

"Fine." She huffed. "I'll look away, you type it in, and then I'll set up the content. You can watch me the whole time." She stood. Walked off.

Keys clicked behind her. She struggled to hold her temper. He didn't know her. Had no reason to trust her. But like it or not, he was stuck with her. For at least two months.

Maybe longer if he decided to stick around and run his half of the dude ranch.

"Okay."

"We'll need to keep a watch on the other dude ranches." She strolled back to the desk, reclaimed the chair.

"And match all their offers, too?"

"Not necessarily, but we need to stay ahead of the game. Make sure we compete. Find things to draw guests here instead of the dozen other ranches they could stay at. Maybe add new features and activities."

"Like what?" He pulled a chair beside her, the legs screeching across the hardwood.

"Pumpkin patches and corn mazes are popular."

"Maybe next year. We've missed the planting season this year."

"Miniature golf courses are big. Or maybe outdoor bowling lanes. We need things that appeal to everyone, not just horse lovers."

"You're good at this stuff."

A compliment? Was that a nugget of grudging respect she saw in his eyes?

"I minored in marketing." She turned to the computer. "Wow. How long's it been since the website has been updated?"

"Eden took care of that." The muscles along his jaw clenched. His glossy eyes reflected the powdery blue of his shirt. So much like Eden's, changing from a myriad of green to blue shades, depending on what she'd worn.

"Listen. I know you don't know me from Adam. But I loved your granny. And your sister."

"I did, too." His tone was defensive, as if he'd cornered the market on loving his lost family members.

"Eden left a huge hole in my life. No, we didn't live close or get to spend time together often, but we were great friends. Whenever I needed to vent about something my family couldn't handle, I called Eden. She often used me as a sounding board, too. I miss that." Her voice caught. "Miss her."

His throat convulsed. "Me, too."

"What do you say we miss her together? Run this place together, honor her memory."

He wanted to. It was there in his eyes. "We'll see. I'll do whatever it takes to keep *my family legacy* in *my family.*"

Squelching a sigh, she turned to the screen. He leaned close, then stood and eased up behind her. His woodsy cologne did a number on her senses. How could such an annoying, combative man smell so good? Not to mention, look so good.

As she added their new special rates and updated content on the website, he watched every move over her shoulder as if she planned to put in one price, then charge a higher rate and pocket the difference.

Her hands shook under his close scrutiny.

"Look good to you?" She waited while he inspected the changes she'd made.

"I approve."

"I'll do some research on the rest of our competition." She logged out. "See what else we can do. Run some ideas by you."

She'd just have to work harder. Prove her dependability. Earn his trust. If they were going to end up as business partners indefinitely, they needed to at least be amicable toward each other.

Landry scanned the bathroom, removed her latex gloves and sanitized her hands. The fixtures, floor and mirror sparkled.

Moving on to the bedroom, she snapped the top sheet in place with military precision, smoothed out every wrinkle and pulled the quilt and bedspread straight.

Day four and she'd found a routine. Mornings were for cleaning. Afternoons for cooking. Evenings for checking the competition. Reservations and tending to guests fell in whenever needed.

Along with trying to win Chase over. Get him to trust her. Whatever it took to ease their tense working situation. Even though she didn't feel like she was getting anywhere with him.

With a skim of the lamb's wool duster over the log lamp, wooden blinds and horseshoe knickknacks, she blew out a heavy breath and surveyed the tidy room. Satisfied, she picked up the plastic-handled tote loaded with cleaning supplies and exited the room. And smacked right into something solid.

Chase. Again.

She dropped the bin. Bottles and supplies bounced and rolled.

"Whoa." Strong hands clutched her upper arms. "We have to stop meeting like this."

"Sorry." Her face steamed. "Still can't seem to watch where I'm going."

They knelt, picked up items, knees almost touching, hands grazing a few times as they stashed everything back in the carrier.

As she stood, he chased down a few strays, handed them to her.

"We all ready for our corporate newlyweds?" He checked his watch. "They should arrive any minute."

"Suite cleaned, stocked with extra towels. Are they returning guests?"

"Not sure." He ushered her in front of him toward the three stories' worth of stairs. "Some company made the reservation. Footing the bill for two weeks."

"They must be at the top of the corporate ladder." She put it in gear to keep from holding him up. "We need to make extra sure they enjoy their stay so they return or at least tell others about us."

"That's our goal with all of our guests." His tone came out gruff as they reached the foyer. "After we get them settled, I could use your help. The slow toilet has turned into a stopped-up one in the Trail Boss Room."

Nice move. Surely he could handle blocked plumbing on his own, yet he seemed determined to share the dirty jobs with her. As if she'd give up her claim because some of the responsibilities meant getting messy. But he wouldn't get rid of her that easily.

He looked out the front window. "Uh, from the looks of things, I doubt they'll be taking any trail rides or fishing trips."

Landry eased up beside him. The couple was

barely out of their car, and already holding hands, staring all moony eyed at each other. Her cheeks warmed.

"Stop spying and get the door for them." She rolled her eyes, grabbed a feather duster out of the cleaning closet and went to work on a spotless shelf.

Why had she and Kyle never shared that type of loving devotion? He'd reserved his affections for when he didn't like what she was saying.

Chase opened the door and said, "Welcome to Chasing Eden Dude Ranch."

She turned around to greet their guests.

"Thank you." The pink-cheeked bride looked around. "This place is cool." But her eyes didn't stray away from her husband for long. Absolutely besotted with each other.

Becca approached from the kitchen.

"Becca will show you to the Lassoed by Love Room on the third floor, and I'll get your luggage." Chase stepped out, grabbed their baggage.

"This way." Becca led them toward the stairs.

"Thank you."

Landry waited until they disappeared up the stairs, then gathered a few supplies from the maintenance closet and headed up to the second level. She'd show Chase she knew her way around a plunger.

She slid her key card in the slot, opened the door.

The faux cowhide bedspread cinched the Trail Boss as the favored room for business executives.

Within five minutes, she'd located the problem and removed it. Minutes ticked past. Where was Chase? Surely he'd settled the newlyweds by now. She perched on the side of the tub. Still, listening, waiting.

A key clicked in the lock.

Showtime. She flushed the commode.

"No!" Booted footfalls went into high gear and he bolted through the door.

She looked up at him with a satisfied grin.

"It'll flood." He jerked the plunger out of her hand.

The water level in the toilet swirled danger-ously high. High enough to make her second-guess herself. But then it drained with a whoosh that matched her expelled breath.

"How did you do that?" His jaw dropped as he set his tool down. "I tried the plunger. Three times. I thought I'd have to turn the water off and pull the commode up to find the blockage."

"Well, it's a good thing I got it, because I've seen how you turn water off."

His mouth twitched.

She held her hand up—still encased in a long latex glove, a big, rusty belt buckle with the image of a bucking bronc in her palm. Probably won at a rodeo.

"You reached down there and pulled that out?"

"It's not my first rodeo." She dropped the buckle in a baggy, set it on the counter as if it was all in a day's work.

"I believe one of our guests reported that missing a few months ago."

"Something tells me he won't be wanting it back." She tugged her glove off, dropped it in a trash bag. "You'd think he'd have heard it clank in there before he flushed."

"Good job." He ground out the compliment with a frown for good measure. "Be sure and disinfect before you prepare food for our guests," he said as he stalked out of the bathroom.

Her smile widened as she soaped disinfectant up to her forearms in the sink.

She was a lot tougher than she looked, and Chase Donovan would soon realize that.

Chapter Three

Five days since her arrival, and Landry had risen to every challenge Chase had thrown her way. But he was determined to have her gone. This ranch was his family's legacy, and he wouldn't give that up to some stranger.

Wonder how she'd feel about helping him with a pregnant cow?

Chase ducked inside the shade of the barn. Fresh hay mixed with the scent of animal. The smell alone should be enough to send her packing. By the time the calf was ready to come, he'd probably be on his own.

He probably shouldn't conspire against her today, on a Sunday. But he couldn't help it if the opportunity had presented itself. A grin tugged at his lips as he tapped her number in his contacts.

"Hello, Chase."

"Are you on the rotation to attend church this morning?"

"Um, no. I told your folks there's no rush. I don't want to disrupt anything."

Yet she'd disrupted everything just by showing up here. "Have you ever seen a calf being born?"

"A couple of times."

"Never mind, then." She kept surprising him. "I thought you might want to witness."

"I do. But I guess I should help prepare for the lunch rush."

"We've got it." He heard his mom's voice in the background. "You go. Have fun."

"Where are you?" Landry asked him.

"In the far west corner of the pen behind the barn. Wash your hands and arms up just in case." That should give her pause.

"I'll be there in five." No hesitation in her voice.

He ended the call. Slid his phone in his pocket, stepped inside the barn to get supplies, took them out near the cow and then went back in to wash up.

As he finished preparations, he heard footfalls and walked outside, his hands held up in the air like a surgeon waiting for a nurse to cover them with gloves. The cow lay on her side, where he'd left her.

"She's been at it awhile. I might have to pull it," he said to Landry as she approached.

"My hands are smaller. Let me, if it comes to that."

"You've done this before?"

"Once." She kept up with his hurried pace. "Do you have a head gate to restrain her?"

"We do, but she's already down. She's tame and this isn't her first calf, so we should be good to go."

What else was this woman capable of? She was nothing like his sister, who cringed and gagged over baiting her own fish hook.

"How long has she been like this?" Landry asked.

"I knew she was ready a few hours back, and she lay down an hour ago." As they neared the cow, he saw one hoof. Only one.

"That means the elbow is caught." She ran her left hand down the russet-colored hide.

He was completely stumped, couldn't believe she actually knew that. "That just happened during the time I went to call you."

"We're here to help you, hon." She looked up at Chase. "Does she have a name?"

"Penelope. The gloves and lubricant are in the top of the supply box."

"Okay, Penelope." She picked up the poly sleeve, slid her right hand into it. It was so long, it wadded up around her shoulder. "Let's get down to business."

Penelope flinched, moaned a weak moo as Landry went to work.

"I know, Penny. It's okay. I'm just gonna see what's going on." She gritted her teeth. "Poor girl. You're already hurting and I'm making it worse. Pet her, Chase."

"Feel anything?" He ran his fingers along the cow's neck. "Do you know what to do?"

"There we go. I freed the elbow." She pulled off her glove and patted Penelope's hip. "Do your stuff, girl." She turned to Chase. "Let's give her a little privacy."

He was in awe. She really knew the ropes. "We need to keep an eye on things."

"Over by the barn. She'll relax better."

He followed, then settled beside her. Tried to cram his growing respect for her down. Just because she knew her way around a ranch didn't mean he wanted her owning half of his.

She caught him staring. "What?"

"Who are you, Landry Malone?"

She grinned. "I grew up on a ranch with cattle, worked at a dude ranch for years, and my cousin is a vet. I watched my first calf birth at nine, saw my first pull at twelve, pulled one at seventeen."

"So, your folks own a Christian bookstore and a ranch?" Sounded like her family had plenty. Like she didn't need to scam anyone.

"The ranch belongs to my grandparents. I spent lots of time there."

"You're nothing like Eden."

"No." Her gaze stayed on Penelope, but her smile widened. "Your sister didn't like to get dirty, hated the smell of farm animals and was afraid of worms."

"Don't tell me. Y'all went fishing and you had to bait her hook?"

"Every time."

"Me, too." What could Eden have had in common with her? "What made y'all friends?"

"I guess she reminded me of my sister." She turned to face him, frowned. "And Eden said I reminded her of you. Not sure if that was a compliment."

He chuckled. "She probably just meant the outdoorsy thing." Landry wasn't afraid to get dirty, but that didn't affect her femininity. He almost wanted to apologize for giving her a hard time. Almost wanted to trust her. But just because she could release a calf, it didn't mean she wasn't out to get his inheritance.

"Maybe we could go fishing sometime."

"Maybe."

"The other foot just came." Her awed whisper caught him off guard.

He'd forgotten all about poor Penelope.

Within an hour they had the calf standing.

"So sweet." Teary-eyed, Landry watched the calf find its legs, the mama nuzzling it along. "Can I name her Petunia?"

"Go for it."

This was supposed to have tested her mettle. But again, she'd risen to his challenge. He couldn't let his guard down, though. He had to shake her down if he wanted to keep his family's

ranch in the family. Not in the hands of the interloper his sister had forced on him.

By lunchtime, Chase's stomach growled as he
smelled the aroma of garlic, onion and tomato
sauce drifting from the kitchen. But he didn't have
time to stop and eat. Monday brought lots of errands to run.

From looking at Landry Malone, dainty, pris-
tine, girly, he never would've imagined her will-
ingly tackling messy jobs. Nor could he have
redone the website if he'd tried. He'd have to do
better if he planned to trip her up today. But he
was running out of ideas.

In the kitchen, his parents and Landry wore
matching food prep hats while they worked.

Mom cleaned the buffet warmer. Dad scrubbed
the grill. Landry disinfected the counter, a smile
on her face. As if they'd worked together for years.
A team. And they had been, several years ago.
Back when he'd let his family down—done his
traveling thing—Landry had been here to pick up
his slack.

But the only thing he knew for certain about her
was that she was beautiful. Even with her wavy
mane covered by the goofy-looking cap.

He looked over at his mother and saw that she
was measuring him. "Have you eaten lunch?"

"I'll grab something in town." He cleared his

throat. "I have to pick up the new bedspread and run several errands. Need anything?"

Both his parents shook their heads.

Landry bit her lip. "Could I come along?"

No. He did not want to haul her around. "Sure."

"I need a few things, and I can't really remember the layout of the town. Is there a Walmart?"

He chuckled. "Thirty minutes away in either Boerne or Kerrville. We have a Dollar General and a grocery store."

"That'll work. Just let me get my purse." She hurried past him, leaving a cloud of flowery perfume mixed with fruity shampoo in her wake. Despite the fact that she'd cooked manicotti and a host of other spicy dishes for lunch.

He followed and waited in the foyer while she went to Granny's private quarters. A few minutes later she was back, her purse slung over her shoulder.

"I'm ready." She'd pulled her hair into a ponytail. He'd never been a fan of the style, but she made it look good.

"Let's go." He strolled to the door, opened it for her.

Once in the truck, her flowery smell intensified. His vehicle would never be the same.

"So, tell me how you came to live here for a while." He chanced a glance at her, then backed out of his parking spot. "Back when you were in culinary school with Eden?"

"They never told you?"

"Might have." He pulled onto the highway. "But I probably wasn't listening. It's a guy thing."

"At least you admit it." She snickered. "I learned a long time ago—if you don't talk about trucks, sports, business or livestock, men don't listen."

"Brothers?"

"No. Just a sister. A dad. Male cousins. Ranch-hand coworkers."

"Isn't Aubrey close to Dallas?"

She kept her eyes on the road. "It is, and I could have gone to school in Dallas. But I was eighteen years old and had never been away from home. I wanted to spread my wings, so I chose the San Antonio option."

"And Eden invited you to live at the dude ranch?"

"Not exactly. I saw her in class, but we didn't ever meet." Her voice filled with reverence when she mentioned his sister. "I had an apartment with a roommate, but our lifestyles didn't gel. I needed a job, and despite wanting to experience independence, I was lonely."

"Not once you met Granny, I bet." Granny always took in strays.

"Definitely not." She stared out the passenger window. "I saw a help wanted ad for a dude ranch, so I called the number and officially met Eden and Granny. I ended up working for room and board for a year and a half until I finished school. They were like my family away from family. And the dude ranch was home away from home."

But they weren't her family. It wasn't her home.

"What happened to all the trees?"

Dead or dying live oaks lined each side of the road. "Oak wilt. It transfers from tree to tree through the root system. Takes no prisoners, doesn't stop until everything in its path is dead."

"That's so sad. I always loved driving through this area with the twisted, gnarled trees."

"Looked like they'd stood up to the dry, rocky Texas hillsides for decades and could survive anything. But not oak wilt," he said as he turned onto Main Street.

"Wow. That was quick." She scanned the storefronts lining the highway. Ancient rockwork buildings, motorcycles and cars parked in front of each, people strolling along, unhurried. "I could have walked here."

"I have to go to the log furniture store, get gas for the tractor and hit the hardware store." He parked halfway between his three destinations. "You can look around if you want." He checked his watch. "And meet me back here at four."

"Is lunch in there somewhere?" Her stomach growled and she winced.

"Didn't you just cook half the day?"

"I can't eat when I'm cooking. Too many smells."

"I was gonna just grab something on the go."

He climbed down from the truck. "But tell you what. Let me go to the furniture store, and then we'll do lunch. Go look around and I'll call you when I'm ready."

She met him on the sidewalk, stood there like a lost puppy. "Can I just hang with you?"

What? "It'll be boring."

"But I don't know a soul here. You can introduce me around. I promise not to get in the way."

"You lived here for eighteen months." He did not need her tagging along. Looking pretty. Smelling good. Vulnerability shining through. All tempting him to trust her motives. "There are probably folks you knew still around."

"I never came to town when I lived here except for church. I worked, studied and went to school. Period."

He squashed a sigh. "Let's get moving, then."

"Thanks." She grinned like he'd just given her the exact gift she'd wanted on Christmas morning.

Landry could hardly take it all in as she followed Chase through the store. A log dining table with a massive slab of wood for the surface. A log dresser with tree bark drawers. A rocker with a massive log frame and thick, comfy cowhide cushions. She'd thought she'd seen it all at the ranch house. She'd been wrong.

But she couldn't let herself get distracted. She'd tagged along for the sole purpose of making Chase realize she was a good person—not the interloper he seemed to think she was. She wanted to make him realize running the dude ranch with her wasn't so bad after all.

"Resa's usually in the office. You can come with me. Or look around." He headed to the back of the store.

Resa? Not a common name. The Resa she knew? At a log furniture store? It had to be.

"Chase, there you are." Landry caught a glimpse of long, dark hair as a woman hugged him. "I'm so glad you're here."

The voice sounded right. Landry jockeyed for a better glimpse, but Chase followed the woman down a hallway.

Minutes ticked past.

"It's perfect. I hope our guests will like it." His voice neared.

Landry ran her hand along a log desk. How could something that used to be a tree be smooth as glass?

"A few may complain, but you can always put them in another room or change bedding. I've never had any bad comments from customers on our display." The woman became visible first. All porcelain skin and contrasting raven hair. Resa. Eden's friend.

Her thousand-watt smile turned on Landry. "Landry, it's so good to see you."

"Yes." She couldn't come up with anything else

as Resa engulfed her in a hug. A mix of emotion wadded in her throat. Relief in knowing someone, an ally in this town, and grief because the last time she'd seen Resa had been at Eden's wedding.

"Y'all know each other?" Chase's frown could have wilted a prickly pear cactus.

"We became friends through Eden." Resa pulled away. "I was studying drafting, living in San Antonio, while they were in culinary school. We'd meet for lunch at least once a week."

"Your dream came true." Landry scrounged up a smile. "You're the fastest furniture slinger in the west."

Resa laughed. "Something like that."

"You own this place?"

"My parents do."

"I remember now." Her parents owned a store in San Antonio and this one here in Bandera. And lived next to the dude ranch, Eden and Resa had been lifelong friends.

"What are you doing here?"

"Landry's my new partner in the ranch." The resignation in Chase's voice made her glance at him. But his features were unreadable.

"Of course. Eden's friend. Why didn't I realize that when Chase was in here—" Resa linked arms with her. "Don't let him scare you. He's all bluster."

What had Chase said about her? "I love the store. I can't believe I never visited before."

"We were too busy studying." Resa rolled her

eyes. "I'm so glad that part of our lives is over. Except for—" She leaned her temple against Landry's, and her sad tone gave away that she was obviously missing Eden. "We should do lunch sometime. I live at my folks' place right next to the Donovan property, so we should be able to get together."

"How about now?" Suddenly lunch with a surly Chase was more than she could handle.

"I'd love to. But I already ate, and I have an appointment with a client." Resa checked her watch. "He should be here any minute."

"We'll get out of your hair, then." Chase's large hand settled in the small of Landry's back.

A shiver went through her.

Not because of him, she told herself. Just at the unexpected touch. Yes, that was it.

"Is he playing nice?" Resa jabbed a finger at him.

"I've been a perfect gentlemen."

Except when you doused me with water. Forced me to unstop a toilet. Used a calf to try to scare me off.

"You call me if he turns ornery." Resa handed her a business card. "Or for lunch." She gave Landry one last hug, waved at Chase as he urged her toward the door.

"Chase, how's it going?" A gray-haired gentleman sat on the church pew outside the store. His skin leathery, a knife in one gnarled hand, an ornate wooden candlestick in the other.

"Things are good. I didn't see you when we came in."

"Just got here. Arthritis is acting up something fierce this morning." His eyes cut to Landry. "Who's the pretty lady? Got yourself a girlfriend, do ya?"

"No." Landry's face heated as her denial blended with Chase's.

"Hmm." The man's eyes narrowed. "Methinks they doth protest too much."

"My Shakespeare-quoting friend here is Jed Whitlow, the best woodcarver in Bandera. This is Landry Malone, my new business partner."

Was it just her imagination, or did Chase's tone turn sour whenever he said that? Like he'd gotten the bitter edge of a pecan hull in his mouth.

"It's nice to meet you, sir."

Jed set his knife down, clasped Landry's hand with surprising strength in his calloused grip. "You, too, young lady. You keep my friend here in line." He winked at Chase. "She don't seem so bad."

"Let's go." Chase set his hand in the small of her back again, propelling her toward the restaurant.

Apparently the whole town knew that Landry had usurped Chase's inheritance. And that he wasn't happy about it. She'd just have to change everyone's mind. Even his. No matter how hard he made it.

* * *

All Chase had to do was get through the rest of his errands with Landry in tow.

The waitress took their drink orders, then scurried away. Old Spanish Trail, or OST, as the locals called it, was Chase's favorite restaurant. It always stirred memories of coming to town for breakfast with Gramps.

"This place is so cool." Landry scanned the room.

Chase looked around with fresh eyes at the enormous elk behind the breakfast bar—where servers had to duck underneath the creature to deliver plates to patrons seated on saddle-topped stools—the covered-wagon salad bar, and the John Wayne Room practically wallpapered with pictures and memorabilia celebrating the Duke.

"When I was a kid, on rare occasions when the dude ranch didn't have guests, Gramps used to bring me here for breakfast."

"I wish I could have known him."

"He's been gone since I was fifteen."

"I'm sorry." She touched his hand. "You've had a lot of loss."

His gaze dropped to their hands.

She pulled hers away, opened her menu. "What's good here?"

"Everything."

Their waitress brought their teas, then took their

order of eggs, bacon and pancakes for Chase and a cheeseburger for Landry .

"Still got it?" The gruff voice startled him.

Chase looked up at the older man who'd spoken to him, then dug in his pocket and laid a knife on the table.

"Gave him that knife when he was a young whippersnapper," the elder continued. "Couldn't have been more than seven." His ring-around-the-head hair stood in downy tufts on the sides, looking much like koala bear ears.

"This is Wallace Kern. He was Gramps's friend."

"I told him not to lose that knife when I gave it to him, and he hasn't let me down yet."

"It's gotten me out of a lot of scrapes."

"This your girlfriend?"

"No." Again they protested together.

"Landry is my new business partner."

"Ohhhh, so this is her." Wallace scrutinized her. "Looks harmless enough. Not like some scammer or con artist."

Landry's face went scarlet. "You never know. Sometimes those types of folks look pretty ordinary."

Wallace guffawed. "I like this one. She's got spunk." He shoved his hands in his overalls pockets, rocked back on his heels. "I better be getting home to the missus. Nice meetin' ya, Miss Landry." Wallace shuffled off.

"So, I guess you complained about me to everybody in town before I got here."

"Not everybody. Just one somebody who apparently has loose lips."

"I'm not a scammer." Something in her eyes tugged at him.

"I sincerely hope not."

"I never imagined Eden would leave me her share of the dude ranch. I never thought she'd—die." She looked down at the table. "Yes, I loved my years here, and I love the dude ranch. Yes, living here planted my dream of owning my own someday. But my own." Her gaze latched on to his. "Not yours."

The waitress brought their food. Despite the swirling tension, he prayed over their meal, and they fell into silence. Their conversation not bothering their appetites at all.

He wanted to believe her. To trust her. But his family legacy was at stake.

Yet the thing in her eyes that tugged at him—it was hurt.

Chapter Four

"I'll do my shopping now." Landry hesitated as they stepped outside the restaurant. "Maybe check out a few stores."

"Suit yourself. Meet me at the truck at four thirty, since we took time to eat." Chase hurried toward the crosswalk leading to the hardware store. Apparently happy to dump her dead weight.

She'd invited herself along to make him like her. Instead his constant distrust was wearing her thin. She needed a break.

He thought she was a scammer. And half the town knew his fears. Maybe all of them. Would she ever belong?

The Dollar General was on the other side of the furniture store. She retraced her steps. How could she feel so alone as she sidestepped numerous people on the bustling sidewalk?

As she neared the pew in front of the furniture store, Jed patted the seat beside him. "Come sit a spell."

Would he chew her out for horning in on Chase's

inheritance? Jed's smile offered nothing other than kindness.

"I guess I have a few minutes." She settled beside him, her feet surrounded by wood shavings, the scent of cedar in the air. "How long have you carved?"

"Long as I can remember." He never looked up from the wood—smoothing with his knife as he twirled the candlestick. "My pappy taught me when I was knee-high to a grasshopper. I used to have a pretty big business with Resa, stocking my work in her store."

"Do you still have items on display? I thought I saw some things that might be yours."

"A few walking sticks and candleholders." His hands never stilled. "But this arthritis slows me. Resa's been good to me."

"She's a really nice person. I met her back when I was going to culinary school." Landry remembered Eden saying Resa didn't date. "Did she ever marry? Have kids?"

"Nope. Just focuses on her furniture designing and the business. It's a shame. She's as pretty on the inside as out."

"Yes, she is." Apparently nothing had changed. "Well, I'd better get my shopping done. It won't make Chase like me any better if he has to wait on me."

"He's a tough one. Doesn't trust easy. But you really can't blame him."

Probably shouldn't ask. Shouldn't inquire into Chase's personal life. But she had to work with him, and knowing what made him tick might make it easier.

Anticipation weighed heavy in her chest. "Why's that?"

"Back when Granny was sick, Chase came home. I reckon every gold digger in the vicinity knew he'd inherit the dude ranch soon. Suddenly he was the most eligible bachelor in Bandera."

No wonder Chase thought she was a scammer. "Everyone here seems to know he thinks I'm the same way."

"There's this girl—been hot on his trail again since Eden's death. She caught him on a bad day, and he said something like, he already had one gold digger on his hands and didn't need another."

"Great." She huffed out a sigh. "The whole town hates me."

"Nah. And if they do, they won't after they meet you. Even Chase. Give him time—he'll warm up to you."

But would he? She hoped so. For the sake of the dude ranch.

And what if she did gain his trust? Could they successfully run a dude ranch together? For life?

So far all of her efforts to win him over had splatted belly up on the pavement. For this to work, they at least had to become friends. She had to find a way—find a chink in Chase's armor. But she was running out of steam. And ideas.

Silence prevailed in the office as Landry scanned reservations on the computer. The day spent sparring with Chase yesterday had done nothing to ease their relationship. Currently he was sprawled in a nailhead chair with his laptop. Perfectly content to ignore her as he went over their supply inventory.

"We had two calls from guests wanting to cancel, but once I told them about our summer special, they kept their reservations." Landry glanced at him. "And I sent out our first newsletter to each of our cancellations about our summer special. They all came back."

He frowned. "We can't spam our guests."

Why was he always so intent on disapproving of anything she did? She held her breath, counted to ten.

"I didn't. They were return guests, and Eden had already signed them up to receive email notifications."

"Oh." The line between his brows smoothed. "Sounds like your idea worked. Good job. Got anything else?"

A compliment and a challenge all wrapped in one. "Back when I lived here, Granny allowed a few neighbors to get married here. My sister is a wedding planner. She could help us turn this place into a sought-after venue."

"And girlie up the ranch?" He set his laptop down, strolled to the window. "After investing in all this log furniture and rustic decor? No way."

"We wouldn't have to change a thing. Rustic is in for weddings. Especially in Texas."

"I have a better idea." He turned to face her. "I just watched five axis deer grazing at the edge of the woods. We could offer corporate hunts. Bring in more exotics."

"Hunting?" Her voice rose an octave. "I'm not turning hunters loose on Bambi's daddy. They already got his mom."

"Um. You know—"

"Bambi's not real. But those poor innocent deer out there are." She jabbed a finger at the window with a shudder. "And I know all the arguments. Axis aren't even native to Texas. They're overpopulated and taking over our native whitetail. There's no season on them and they have huge horns, so hunters love them."

"They're called racks, not horns. How do you know so much about them?"

"Our main competitor for the Aubrey ranch where I worked offered exotic hunts. But we found other ways to boost business." She leveled her gaze on him. "How would you like to be hunted?"

"You sound like Eden." Something in his eyes softened. "And Granny."

It was his family legacy. But he knew as well as she did, Eden and Granny would go for weddings rather than have hunters traipsing over the property. She'd even heard Granny mention how she'd always made her own husband go elsewhere for his hunting expeditions.

"So, let's get this straight. You have issues with hunting, but you grew up on a ranch. You eat beef."

"And I eat venison. But I don't want anything to do with killing the animal."

He tried to hold his laughter, but it rolled out. A deep, warm sound.

And Landry laughed with him.

Were they having a moment?

He seemed to realize it and immediately stopped laughing. He went back to his chair and settled once again with his laptop.

She forced her gaze away from him, back to the screen.

The phone rang and Landry jumped, then answered. "Chasing Eden Dude Ranch. How may I help you?"

"My name is Consuelo Sanchez. I know it's short notice, but our family vacation time got moved up a week. Do you have any rooms available?"

"Let me check for you, Mrs. Sanchez." Landry tried to infuse her smile into her tone. "How many, and when do you plan to arrive?"

"That's the really crazy part. We'd get there tomorrow. Six adults and six kids." Landry heard young voices in the background. "I saw a room on y'all's website. It looks like a big old great room with a TV and a bunch of bunk beds built into the wall. Could we get something like that, only with adult beds, too?"

"That's the Tumbleweed Room. It has three bunk beds and a sleeper sofa, along with two connecting rooms, the Right as Rain and the Rest a Spell Rooms, with a queen bed in each."

"That sounds perfect." Relief filled the woman's tone.

Landry tried to keep it all business, despite the elation building inside her. "How many nights would you need it?"

"We'll stay a week and check out next Wednesday. Please tell me you have something. We could go three double rooms with two queen beds in each."

"Three rooms would cost less, but the Tumbleweed Room and both connecting rooms are available."

"Oh, that's wonderful. Having the great room will be worth it."

Definitely. Landry confirmed the dates. "I have an all-inclusive package with as many activities such as trail rides, fishing trips and bonfires as you'd like, plus three meals a day for the duration of your stay." She rattled off rates she knew by heart.

"That's just what we're looking for."

Landry could hardly contain her excitement as she entered the lady's info into the computer. "That's everything I need. We'll see you tomorrow."

"Thank you."

"Thank you." Landry pushed End.

"A nice reservation, I take it."

"I just booked the Tumbleweed Room, the Right as Rain Room and the Rest a Spell Room for a week. And there are six kids. They're getting the all-inclusive package."

"Awesome."

Her cell phone rang. She leaned back, dug it out of her pocket, scanned the screen. Devree.

"Hey, sis. How's it going?"

"You were supposed to call me once you got settled in."

"Sorry." She winced. Had completely forgotten. "It's been busy here."

"Are you coming home for your birthday?"

"I'm kind of busy running a dude ranch." Half of one, anyway. "I mean, helping run."

"Are you coming home anytime soon?"

"I'm not sure."

"Tell me about the partner."

"Maybe some other time." Her gaze flitted to Chase. Watching her.

"Oh, so he's there. Is he cute?"

Landry's face heated. She spun her chair, kept her back to him. "I'm sort of busy right now."

"He is, isn't he?"

"Devree. Was there a reason you called?"

Her sister's sigh echoed through the line.

Landry's pulse went up a notch. "Are Mama and Daddy okay?"

"Everybody's fine here. But I have to tell you something, because I don't want you to hear it somewhere else. I don't want to tell you, but you need to know." Her sister always rambled when nervous. "I was hoping to tell you in person."

"Just tell me."

"It's Kyle. He's engaged."

Landry's stomach landed at her feet.

"Are you still there?"

"I'm here." Her voice didn't sound right. It was hollow. Just like her insides.

"I'm sorry, Landry. I just thought you should know."

"It's okay." Kyle had moved on—planned to marry someone else just over ten months after humiliating her at the altar. "It doesn't matter."

"Are you okay?"

"I'm fine. Thanks for telling me, but I need to get back to work now."

"Call me if you need me."

"I will. Love you."

"You, too."

She ended the call, just sat there, staring out the window.

Her insides boiled. But not with hurt. Anger more than anything else.

"Is something wrong?"

She jumped. For once, she'd forgotten all about Chase.

"Nothing. Everything's fine." She kept her back to him. She couldn't process this under his scrutiny. Didn't have the strength to spar with him.

If only she could melt through the floor.

What had her sister said? Obviously something upsetting. Chase watched her. So still.

Minutes passed with her back still toward him. Finally she turned her chair to the desk, her face a blank slate. She stared at the computer screen, moved the mouse, then began typing.

Was it his imagination or had she gone pale? Should he quietly leave the room? Or try to help?

"You sure you're okay?"

"Just tired."

It seemed like way more than that.

"I can handle anything that turns up if you want to turn in." He kept his tone gentle.

"I think I will." She got up and quickly scurried out of the room.

"Good night." Chase stared after her.

He really shouldn't. But curiosity was getting the best of him. He'd seen her stare at the computer when she'd gotten off the phone. Had she looked up something?

It was worth a try. He had to learn what caused that stricken look on her face. He moved to the desk, opened the browser and clicked on History.

Engagement announcements from the state paper. He clicked the link.

Mr. and Mrs. Kyle Reginald Billings Sr. announce the engagement of their son, Kyle Reginald Billings Jr., to Waverly Larissa Heathcott…

The blond preppy guy again. Wow, he'd moved on from Landry in less than a year. With a bombshell blonde this time, though posed almost exactly as he had with Landry. While she'd been preparing to move to the dude ranch, her ex-fiancé had proposed to someone else. And apparently she'd just found out.

That explained things. Was she crying in her room? Alone and upset? What should he do? Ask Mom to check on her?

No. He wasn't supposed to know.

Even though he didn't trust her, didn't want her around, the thought of her anguish tugged at his heart.

The next morning, Chase crossed the office, hesitated in the foyer and glanced inside the great room. It was too early for any of their guests to be up yet. But there was also still no sign of Landry.

He cut through and pressed his ear to the door of her private quarters. Couldn't hear a thing. His grandparents had gone to great lengths to sound-proof the dude ranch for their guests as well as their own privacy.

"Chase?" Mom. In the room.

He closed his eyes, turned around and tried to act normal.

Mom leaned against the doorframe of the great room, her eyebrows arched high.

"I'm concerned about her," he whispered, strolling casually toward his mom. "She found out her ex-fiancé is engaged, but I'm not supposed to know that."

"I won't ask how you found out." A crease formed between Mom's eyes. "I guess that's why her mom called. Her family is coming for her birthday."

"When's her birthday?" She hadn't said a word.

"Friday. Your father's preparing a feast and, of course, a cake. Her sister is arriving tomorrow night and said she'll stay with Landry. Her parents get here Friday morning, and Becca booked them a room. They'll leave Saturday afternoon." Mom's eyes narrowed. "How are things between y'all?"

"Tense hours interrupted by nanoseconds of tranquillity."

"She's a nice girl." Mom patted his shoulder, plopped in a wingback. "Give her a break."

"What do we really know about her?"

Mom rattled off the things he already knew. That she was from Aubrey, was an accomplished chef, had befriended Eden and Granny when she worked here. Mom crossed her legs, bounced her foot as fast as she talked. "And that idiot dumped her at the altar last September."

That—he hadn't known. "So he dumped her. Why?"

"Beats me." Mom shrugged. "I guess because he was a jerk. Poor child. You remember when she came here right before… Eden's wedding."

It was always hard for his family to think about his sister's wedding. It was so tied up with her death, given it was the last time they'd seen her alive.

"I never saw Landry during her stay."

"She was inconsolable. Stayed holed up in her room the entire time. Only dragged herself out for—"

Eden's wedding. Which led to her honeymoon. Which led to her death.

"Why do you think Eden left her share of this place to Landry?"

"Landry loves it here. As much as Eden did."

"But we love it here." He sank into the chair beside her. "And we're family."

"Yes. But your father and I are consumed with

the restaurant. You just want to catch fish, drive cattle and guide the tenderfoots about."

Why did the truth make him sound like an irresponsible, overgrown kid?

"Maybe your sister knew you'd need Landry to take care of the unfun stuff."

"I was doing fine before she came."

"You were." She leaned toward him, patted his knee. "And your father and I are very proud of you. But you don't enjoy the business part of things. With Landry here, you don't have to worry with it."

"You trust her?"

"Completely."

"I just can't let my guard down." He gripped the arms of his chair. "What if her ex-fiancé dumped her because he figured out she was a gold digger? What if she's a scammer and she charmed Eden into handing over our legacy?"

"Landry?" Mom chuckled. "She's salt of the earth. And if she was a scammer, she'd have wrangled your half from Granny, as well." Her eyes turned serious. "Just because Mallori Ferndale and Tiffanie Cardwell came sniffing around a few years back doesn't mean all women are after your inheritance. Landry isn't like them. Really, son, you need to relax."

Tiffanie had still been sniffing until he'd told her off a few weeks ago. Now she was just spreading rumors.

"I know what you need." Mom stood, crossed to the foyer, continued to the kitchen.

When she got in high gear, it was hard for even him to keep up.

In the kitchen, she opened the freezer. "You need to go fishing."

Dad looked up from whatever dish he was prepping. "Our freezer is running low on the fresh catches we advertise on the menu."

And Mom knew just how to relax him. Whiling away the day at the river was exactly what he needed.

"And take Landry with you."

"Huh?" His pulse spiked.

"You need to get to know her better, and if she's upset, fishing will cheer her up."

"Don't you need her in the kitchen?"

"We're fully staffed, and she's quite the fisherman." Dad chuckled. "Even has her commercial license. You need her more than we do."

"If you don't ask her, I will," Mom said. "But not a word about our surprise guests. I'll need you to keep her occupied tomorrow night so her sister's arrival can be a surprise. Now go." Mom waved him away. "Scoot."

Just then he heard car doors slamming. Lots of them. It must be the Sanchez family.

He stood, strolled to the foyer and saw Becca standing at the open door.

The smallest girl, probably about five, bounced

up the sidewalk. Her frilly dress revealed bruised and bandaged knees. Probably how Landry looked at that age. Two more girls and three boys ranging in age up to ten or so. Bringing up the rear, a middle-aged couple, and two other couples in their late twenties or early thirties. The men of the group and Ron were loaded down with luggage.

Chase hurried to assist. "Let me help."

"We got it all," the oldest man said but allowed Chase to take some of his burden.

"Mommy, can we do the bonfire now?" the tomboy whined.

"It's too hot for that, punkin. We'll have lots of fun things to do here, but let's get settled in our room first. Then maybe we can go swimming."

As the throng entered the dude ranch, the kids got even more excited, pointing out the rustic fixtures.

"Maybe we can have a hot dog roast over the fire pit without scorching ourselves during your stay." Chase tried to stay focused on the family, but his thoughts pinged back to Landry.

"We'll show you to the Tumbleweed Room." Ron took over for him. "It connects to the Right as Rain Room and the Rest a Spell Room."

"This place is great." The older woman's accent echoed her Hispanic heritage as she looked around, mouth agape.

"All of the log furnishings came from a local maker." Chase rattled it all off, devoid of emotion, on autopilot. "All made from Texas trees. And the fabrics and decor are from a Texas designer. There are brochures in each room if you're interested."

"We'll have to check it out while we're here."

"Would you like lunch? I can put orders in."

"Thank you, but we stopped to eat. We'll be fine until supper."

The horde climbed the stairs with everyone talking at once. Chase followed the family, his mind firmly on the prospect of fishing with Landry.

He didn't want to get to know her. Didn't want to cheer her up. She was possibly a con artist. Or vulnerable and on the rebound. Either way, he needed to avoid her at all costs.

Landry knew she should go help with lunch preparations. Instead, she twirled the office chair from side to side, staring at the picture of Kyle and his fiancée on the screen. Probably the same photographer he'd used with Landry. She focused on his face. Waited for her heart to squeeze or stab. Nothing.

Her fists clenched. The photo just made her mad. That was all. Especially since her replacement was so gorgeous. Tons of perfectly waved hair, stunning blue eyes, sun-bronzed complexion, not a freckle in sight. It really wasn't fair.

Yet why couldn't she cry? Her ex-fiancé—a man she'd loved and planned to marry until he mumbled an apology and dashed out of the church—

had proposed to someone else. But she remained dry-eyed.

When he'd dumped her, had he killed her love for him? Or had she never really loved him at all? Her stomach turned. She closed the browser.

There had been niggling doubts about her relationship with Kyle. The way he'd tried to change her wardrobe and transform her into business casual. The way he'd bought her a makeover and tried to glam her up. It made sense. He'd tried to transform her into what he wanted. What he had now.

Truth be known, Landry hadn't been satisfied with him, either. He hated all the outdoorsy stuff she loved. He'd refused to go horseback riding, hiking or even on a picnic with her. And after she'd told him about her dream of owing a dude ranch, he'd insisted on upgrading and buying a bed-and-breakfast instead. To top things off, he'd belittled her and hijacked their wedding.

Only two things were certain. No man would ever get the chance to dump her again. Ever. And obviously, she wouldn't know love if it kicked her in the teeth. Best to avoid men entirely.

Her insides gave a lonely twist, and she knew why. Because deep down, she still wanted someone to love, marriage and children. Maybe she should have waited until after her birthday to come here. She'd never spent one away from her family. Not even when she'd been in culinary school.

"Want to go fishing?" Chase asked.

She jumped.

"Sorry. I thought you heard me come in."

"I'd love to go fishing." Relax and while away her day. But with Chase? "I need to help your folks with lunch, though."

"I've been instructed to refill the freezer with fish. Dad seems convinced you're a great fisherman and I should take you along. So, you any good?"

"I have my moments." She lifted an eyebrow. "I fished Eden under the table every time we went."

"No offense, but that didn't take much." The corners of his mouth twitched. "Show me what you got. Permission granted from the kitchen. All our staff is in full force."

"I don't know." She nibbled her lip. Fishing always soothed her, but nothing about Chase put her at ease. Yet she needed to get out of her funk. "I might put you to shame." She needed to get back to endearing herself to him. Focus on successfully running the dude ranch with him.

"Give it your best shot."

"You're on. Let me change clothes." She hurried to her quarters. Maybe this outing would drown her confusion over Kyle.

Five minutes later, dressed in worn jeans and an oversize T-shirt, with her hair in a ponytail, she found Chase waiting in the foyer.

"You are, hands down, the fastest female in the West."

She winced. "Translate that to—takes little time with her appearance."

"Some women's appearances don't need time." Her eyes widened. Was that a compliment?

"Eden was like that. But she never realized it." He opened the door, ushered her out. "She fussed and fluffed when she didn't need to."

"I always wished I had her coloring. With her olive skin, you couldn't tell when she was blushing or steaming. She was just always gorgeous."

"Blushing and steaming can be cute, though."

Was he flirting with her? No. Just being nice. For a change.

"Here's our gear." Piled on one side of the porch.

"I can get some of it." She ended up with the two poles and the tackle box, while he carried two coolers.

"Are you up for a hot dog roast tomorrow night? I promised the Sanchez kids."

"I love hot dogs. And s'mores. Count me in."

"A chef who appreciates hot dogs?"

"Hey, I became a chef because I'm a foodie. It doesn't have to be fancy as long as it's good. And hot dogs are sooo good. But the chef thing comes in handy—I can clean our catch, too."

"I'd take you up on that, but since we serve them in the restaurant we have to get them processed by a commercial fishmonger."

"I know." She rolled her eyes. "Pesky rules."

Various birds chirped and sang as they strolled the thirty yards to the river, shrouded in a comfortable silence. Once they reached the bank, they set their gear down and went to work baiting their hooks.

Landry chose a fat worm, slid it onto her hook.

"Impressive, Malone. Apparently you have no qualms being party to an earthworm's death."

"They're slimy and gross." She scrunched her nose up.

"Let me guess—the same reason you have no problem contributing to the death of fish."

"Exactly. And they taste so good."

"Full of contradictions, aren't you?"

"Shh, you'll scare the fish away."

He chuckled, baited his hook, moved up the river from her a bit.

As the distance widened between them, she started breathing easier. Why was Chase giving her such mixed signals?

He didn't even like her. Did he?

She didn't know about him, but *she* liked this new Chase. Maybe too much.

Chapter Five

Though they'd gotten along fine during their fishing trip yesterday and caught a nice haul, today lifeguard duty had kept Chase busy. And with Landry working in the kitchen, they'd barely crossed paths.

As a plume of smoke rose in the night sky, he set the chairs in a circle around the small fire pit. The flames licked hungrily at the logs, crackling and popping.

A squeal came from the path. Landry led the Sanchez family in his direction. The kids whooped and bounced as if they'd never seen a fire pit before. They probably hadn't, seeing as they were city folk from Waco.

The middle of July temperatures had cooled to the midseventies for the evening. And the children's excitement brought out the kid in him.

Maybe this rambunctious family could keep his mind off Landry. She befuddled the grits right out of him.

He really didn't understand why Mom was so set on Landry being out of the ranch house when her sister arrived. Either way, he was sure Landry would be surprised.

Across from him, he saw her settle in a chair by a table that was loaded with hot dogs, buns, condiments and ingredients for the s'mores.

"How many want hot dogs?" she asked while impaling one with a roasting fork.

All the kids' hands went up with shouts of, "Me. Me. Me."

"Just be careful," she warned both parents and children. "The prongs are sharp. No jousting matches. And they're metal, so they get hot. Be sure to keep your hand on the grip."

She skewered more hot dogs and wisely passed them to one of the adults, leaving the family to make the call whether the kids got to handle their own forks or not. Just as he'd instructed her when going over safety precautions during their fishing expedition.

The fire reflected in her dark chocolate eyes, and he still saw sadness there. He'd have liked to have a serious word with that Kyle yayhoo right about now. Walking out on one woman in the middle of the ceremony, proposing to another ten months later. Who did that?

Despite his best efforts, he cared about her hurt feelings. But he wasn't supposed to be sensitive toward her. He needed to stay on guard.

"How about we sing campfire songs?" Chase cleared his throat. "If you're happy and you know it, clap your feet." He made an attempt and ended up clapping his boot heels.

All the kids laughed, and he even got a chuckle out of Landry.

"That's not how it goes, Mr. Chase." Maria, the little tomboy, giggled.

"You know it?"

She nodded, her braids bouncing.

"Why don't you show us, then?"

The little girl climbed into Landry's lap and sang off-key at the top of her lungs. With a smile, Landry joined in and somehow managed to hit the right notes.

When they ran out of lines, Chase gave the feet-clapping another try, and the kids attempted it, too. Laughter echoed around the fire. Even Landry's. Sometime during their fun, her sadness had melted away. Her smile reached her eyes as she cuddled and joked with Maria. She was really great with the little girl. With all the kids.

So far, she'd pitched right in at the ranch, capable at everything she got involved in, including making guests feel right at home. Somehow, instead of seeing her as a hindrance, he was beginning to think she was exactly what she seemed. And maybe it wasn't so bad having her around, after all.

As Maria slid from her lap and clambered back to her mother, Landry noticed Chase staring at her. Could that be admiration in his eyes? Was he maybe starting to like her?

But then something changed. A bemused smile took over, like he knew something she didn't.

"Roar!" came a yell as someone grabbed her shoulders.

Landry jumped. A scream climbed her throat.

"Sorry, I couldn't resist." Devree leaned her head against Landry's, auburn waves spilling over her shoulder, mixing with her own lighter colored tangle of curls. "It's just me."

The kids dissolved into giggling.

Landry jumped up and hugged Devree. "What are you doing here?"

"I thought I'd surprise you for your birthday tomorrow."

"I can't believe you came." Her eyes stung.

"I hope you have a room for me."

"Of course. You can bunk with me." Landry remembered their audience, turned back to face them. "This menace who just scared me half to death is my sister, Devree."

"Want a hot dog or s'mores?" One of the kids piped up.

"Tempting." Devree patted her stomach, her curious stare landing on Chase. "But I ate before I came."

"This is Chase, Eden's brother."

"It's nice to meet you." Chase caught Landry's gaze across the fire. "So it's your birthday tomorrow. You know what that means?" He winked at one of the kids, then launched into an operatic version of "Happy Birthday."

Everyone soon joined in, and Landry's face heated. She muttered a quick thanks when the song ended.

"I think it's time for the kiddos to head in for the night," Grandma Sanchez said as she covered a yawn.

The kids protested but soon followed the adults to the ranch house.

"Y'all, too. Get lost." Chase waved the sisters off. "Go visit. I'll take care of the clean-up."

"Thanks." Had he decided to play nice for good? Or just because she'd had a rough day and it was her birthday tomorrow?

A night chorus of frogs and crickets serenaded them as Devree linked arms with her and turned toward the main house.

Landry loved her sister, was excited to see her, but she didn't want to deal with the whole Kyle's engagement thing under Devree's scrutiny.

"So, how long are you staying?"

"Until Saturday afternoon. I thought you could use some company."

"That sounds great." Though she wasn't completely convinced of her own words. Her sister knew her too well and would read Landry's mixed-up heart like the bridal magazines Devree's wedding planning thrived on.

"I knew it."

"Knew what?"

"Chase is cute." Devree's sigh echoed down the moonlit path.

"I haven't really noticed."

"Pfft. Have, too. You're brokenhearted, but not dead. Who needs what's-his-name when you've got a cute cowboy at your disposal?"

"We're business partners. That's all."

"Mmm-hmm." Devree rolled her eyes. "I saw the way he was looking at you."

"If he was looking at me at all, it's because you were sneaking up on me."

"Nope. He was all moony-eyed. Come to think of it, you were mooning right back at him when you introduced us."

"He was not. I was not." Landry whacked her sister's arm. "You're imagining things."

Something bolted through the woods to their left.

"What's that?" Devree stopped dead in her tracks.

With their arms still linked, Landry jerked back in midstep and almost crashed into her sister. "Probably a deer."

"You sure?" Devree's voice quivered, her nails biting into Landry's skin.

"I can't believe you were raised in the country." Landry looked up at the stars peppering the sky and the bright half moon lighting the wooded trail. "It's beautiful."

"And creepy." Devree's feet got in gear. She practically dragged Landry the rest of the way to the house.

At least Devree was distracted from the Chase subject. But her sister had come too close to the truth. If she wasn't careful, Chase could light a fire in her heart big enough to warm all of Texas.

Best to avoid any kind of sparks he might ignite.

Luggage. Chase was beginning to dread the sight of luggage. And to long for an escape. A trail ride, a cattle drive, a camping trip. Something. Anything. As long as it was outside. The bright afternoon sunshine taunted him from every window.

At least climbing stairs with suitcases was great exercise, and this new family of four that was checking in traveled lighter than most guests he'd unloaded lately. The kids chattered to their parents nonstop as he followed the troop up the stairs.

"Anything y'all need?" He set the cases down, unlocked the Tough as Nails Room and made sure the connecting door to the Trail Dust Room was open.

"That should do." Mr. Adams set his luggage down, his breath coming fast, his paunchy stomach working against him. "We'll spend most of our days with family and be here only to sleep, so we won't need meals or anything extra."

"We clean, supply fresh towels and restock toiletries daily. If there's something else, just dial the front desk." He set the cases he'd carried inside the room, then exited and headed back downstairs.

Maybe tomorrow he'd be able to get away and at least pick up the fish they'd caught from the market. But today was Landry's birthday and her parents would arrive any minute. It wouldn't kill him to cover for her, so she could enjoy her family. He checked his watch. Should be here anytime.

The front door opened, and a man with a single suitcase shuffled in with a woman following close behind.

"Mama. Daddy." Landry rushed to them with hugs. "What are y'all doing here?"

"You didn't really expect your mother to stay away on your birthday, did you?" Laugh lines creased around the man's kind eyes, the same shade as Landry's.

She definitely got her coloring from her dad, though his hair was more on the orange side.

"I love your new capris." Landry hugged her mom. "You look great."

"I agree." Her dad winked.

Her mom swatted him and shook her head, her graying light brown curls tumbling. Bone structure so much like Landry's.

Then she noticed Chase lurking on the staircase above them.

"Excuse me." He hurried the rest of the way

down, ducking his head, and turned toward the kitchen.

"Wait. Come meet my parents."

He stopped. "Sure."

"This is Chase Donovan. Eden's brother, my business partner."

Chase tipped his hat as Mr. Malone's brown stare bored into him. The look seemed to be a don't-trifle-with-my-girl challenge, making Chase want to fidget. What had Landry told her folks about him?

"Tina Malone." Her mom offered him her hand. "And this glowering teddy bear is Owen."

Owen's face went red, the color immediately clashing with his hair. Landry got her blushing from her dad, too. But she was way prettier when she did it.

"Nice to meet y'all." He clasped hands with Tina, then Owen.

"Did you know about this?" Landry's gaze met his.

"I'm pretty good at keeping secrets."

"I'm so glad y'all are here." She gave her parents a group hug.

"Hey. Y'all made it." Devree entered from the great room and wiggled herself into the embrace.

"Go spend the day with your family," Chase told Landry.

"But we have guests." Landry's voice came from inside the huddle.

"We also have staff. Now, go on. Get outta here." He strolled to the kitchen to check on the birthday dinner she still didn't know about.

Her family had gone to a lot of trouble—taken time away from their store to spend her birthday with her. Driven six hours to get here. Set up a meal of all her favorites with a cake, then planned to turn around tomorrow and return to Aubrey.

Obviously they were a close family. Much like his. More and more, it hit him: Landry was the real deal.

And everything he wanted in a woman. If he let his guard down with her, he might just fall for her. But a one-sided romance with his on-the-rebound business partner would complicate everything. And possibly leave him with a broken heart.

Maybe she wasn't a gold digger after all. But nothing had changed about their situation. He still needed to keep his distance.

"That was awesome. Yum." Landry patted her stomach and glanced around. She was surrounded by her family and the Donovans at a private table in the kitchen. "Thank y'all so much for making my birthday special."

"But wait." Elliot stood, hurried to the massive commercial fridge. "There's more."

"I can't hold any more." She'd already eaten all her favorites. Chicken and dumplings, fried okra, candied sweet potatoes and shoepeg corn casserole.

"You'll wanna make room for this." Mama patted her knee.

A familiar scent wafted through the air. Something burning? Surely not. Elliot was an experienced chef. He didn't burn things.

He returned carrying a layer cake topped with nuts and coconut surrounding her name, which was spelled out in wax-dripping lettered candles, and followed by the numbers 2 and 6. That must be what she'd gotten a whiff of. "Happy birthday to you." Mama started the song as everyone joined in.

Landry's eyes misted. She covered her mouth with her hands as they finished. "I haven't had a cake with my name on it since I was a teenager."

"Let's get a picture before we cut it. Owen, Tina, Devree, squeeze in around her." Janice took several shots with her phone and a digital camera. "I'll make sure y'all get copies."

"Thank you." Surrounded by her family, Landry blinked away her tears. They'd leave in the morning. Without her.

Photo op over, Chase held a plate for his mom while she cut the cake. "Dad's specialty Italian cream cake."

"My favorite." Landry grinned at her mother. "Again."

Chase handed her the plate. Her fingers grazed his as she took it.

"Thanks."

Her face warmed as she felt his gaze on her.

Glancing around the table, she saw everyone's eyes were on her, not just his. Her family was probably drawing conclusions about her and Chase. She'd just have to show them otherwise.

She bit into her slice of the cake. "Mmm." Cream cheese icing, moist, fluffy and delectable. "This is sooo good. Thank you."

Elliot shot her a wink. "You're welcome."

Talk quieted as the gathering dug into their dessert.

Minutes later, Landry polished off her last bite, scraped her fork across the plate to collect stray icing and popped it in her mouth. She stood and started to take her dish to the sink.

"Give me that." Janice whipped it out of her hands. "We'll clean up. Go enjoy the rest of your day with your folks."

"Y'all exceeded my expectations," her mom said as she stood. "Thank you so much for making Landry feel special."

"It was nothing." Elliot gathered dishes, silverware clanking together.

Mama and Devree headed for the great room.

"Come sit with me on the porch swing." Daddy's warm Texas drawl warmed her insides.

Making her homesick and making her dread them leaving in the morning.

Once outside, she claimed one end of the swing. The chains creaked as he settled beside her. She pushed off with her foot, setting the swing in a sideways jerky motion. Kind of like her life.

She was glad her father was here. Daddy always did his best to right things for her. With his arm around her shoulders, she felt safe.

"Sorry about the scoundrel and his shenanigans."

"You've always had such a way with words." She leaned her head against his shoulder. Old Spice and Dial soap filled her senses with comfort. "But I'm really okay—other than being mad and embarrassed. I don't think I really loved him."

"He certainly wouldn't have been my choice. I hate the way it all went down, but I'm glad you didn't end up married to him."

"Me, too." She rose up, looked at him. "How did you know you loved Mama?"

"I couldn't stop thinking about her." Daddy grinned, gazed off in the distance. "I couldn't stand being away from her. She kept me on pins and needles unless we were together."

"That's sweet." She'd never felt that way with Kyle. Not even with all his business trips. "I'm glad you and Mama came. It wouldn't have been right without y'all on my birthday."

"Me, too. I wish we could stay longer, but one of my students from Sunday school class is getting baptized tomorrow."

"I'll be fine." She leaned into his shoulder again,

his coarse hair bristly against her temple. "Don't worry."

"I wasn't sure about this Chase fella. But spending time with him and his folks, I'm glad they're here with you. If only I could find somebody reliable for Devree, I might sleep at night."

"Daddy." She rose again. "Chase and I aren't—"

"I know. But I also know he'll watch out for you. Gives me peace."

Having Chase near was anything but peaceful. He sent her nerves into orbit. What would it be like to have him really care about her? Her heart could only dream.

Yet she couldn't allow it to.

Chase stood off to the side as Landry's family gave her one more hug in the foyer.

"I wish y'all could stay the rest of the weekend." Landry's smile didn't quite make it to her eyes.

"We'd love to, sugar plum." Her dad kissed her cheek. "Maybe next time."

"Travel safe."

"We will. Take care of yourself." Her mom patted her cheek.

"Watch out for our girl, Chase." Her dad caught his gaze over her shoulder.

Was that approval in his tone? "Will do."

"You're coming to Ally's wedding. Right?" Devree asked her sister.

"Of course."

Whoever Ally was, Landry looked like attending her wedding was the last thing she wanted to do.

The huddle broke up. She waved as they exited. Once the door shut behind them, she sucked in a shuddery breath and swiped under her eyes.

Her family's visit had gotten to her. And Chase realized *she* was getting to *him*. Her vulnerability spoke to his protective side. First she'd been hurting over her ex-fiancé's engagement. Now she was hurting over her family's departure.

But he couldn't allow himself to get too close. He wouldn't be her rebound guy. Best to keep his distance.

Thankfully it would be easy today since he was scheduled for afternoon lifeguard duty. And Saturdays were usually a busy day at the pool. His cell started up singing out the nostalgic and sappy tune of "Happy Trails."

Landry's weak grin turned into a full-out smirk.

"What?" He dug his phone from his pocket.

"I wouldn't have expected that ringtone from you."

"Our guests like it." He scanned his cell screen. Danny, the other lifeguard. "Hello?"

"Hey, Chase, I'm so sorry." Regret loaded each syllable of Danny's words. "My wife's in labor."

As excuses went... "Well that's the most exciting thing I've heard all day. Go. And keep me posted."

The soon-to-be-dad hung up without even saying bye. Chase blew out a big breath, pocketed his phone.

"Good news?"

"Danny's wife is in labor. He was supposed to be on lifeguard duty with me today."

"I can fill in."

His gaze swung to hers. "You're certified?"

"When I first hired on at the dude ranch in Aubrey, they needed a lifeguard, not a chef."

What couldn't she do? "I'll need your certification."

She dug a slim wallet out of her pocket, handed him the laminated card.

"You'll find what you need in the women's locker room." He handed her certification back, recited the locker combination. "Suit up."

"You sound like Captain America."

He snapped his heels together, saluted her.

With a grin, she headed for the exit.

He'd hoped to avoid her. But now he'd spend a day with her. He strolled out to the pool.

Five minutes later, she joined him. "You can take that side." He pointed to the lifeguard chair at the west end of the pool.

She scanned the pool. "No one's here yet."

"They're eating lunch. They'll start pouring in any minute." He checked his watch. "It's Saturday."

"It gets pretty busy, I guess."

"Keeps us hopping."

"Have you ever thought about opening the pool to the public? That way, our facilities would appeal to the community and not just out-of-towners."

Might be a good idea. But... "The pool is a privilege for our guests. I don't want to fill it up with people not even staying here and inconvenience our customers."

"A valid point." She tapped her chin with her finger. "Is there a downtime for the pool, like now?"

"Things get active around eight, when the parents can't contain their kids any longer." He put on his sunglasses as the glare of the sun popped over the ranch house. "It's busy until ten or so. Then kicks back up about noon until three, when it's too hot to do much else. Our guests are in and out from about five to eleven, when we close for the evening."

"So we could open it to the public from ten until noon and then three until five." She shielded her eyes from the sun, looked up at him. "Without inconveniencing our guests?"

"We could. But counting you, we have four certified lifeguards. And two of us pull double and triple duty as trail and fishing guides."

"College kids are always looking for summer jobs. Probably some already certified." She shrugged. "And if we can't find anyone certified, see if any of the staff would be willing. We pay for their classes and we've got extra lifeguards."

"The certification costs almost three hundred dollars."

"Yes. But we charge five dollars for adults and three for kids to swim." She brushed a stray hair away from her face. "Three or four days and we'd recoup our investment. And we could rent out the pool for birthday parties."

"That much—for two hours?"

"For the day. We'll stamp their hands and they can come back for seconds."

"What if we do this and our guests want to swim during public hours?" He adjusted the strap on his whistle.

"They can. Guests get a swimming pass. And drawing locals here will encourage them to mention us to their out-of-town family and friends."

"You might be on to something."

Her whole face lit up as if his approval endorsed her presence. "I know that was hard for you to admit."

A family headed toward them.

"I'll think on it. In the meantime, we need to man our posts." He strolled away from her, rounded the end of the pool and climbed his lifeguard chair.

She was already seated across from him. Her gaze riveted on the water as the family with two small children entered the pool.

Smart. And beautiful. For years, he'd wished he could meet a down-to-earth woman, someone not afraid to get dirty, someone who loved the outdoors as much as he did. Now he finally had. A distracting combination.

Another family with even more kids entered the pool, and Chase refocused. A lifeguard couldn't afford distractions.

And besides, her heart still belonged to the man who'd broken it. Landry Malone was the most off-limits woman he'd ever met.

Chapter Six

Landry settled in the log chair at the check-in counter, her stomach in turmoil.

Sunday morning and she knew Janice would be along to see her soon. She needed to get out of going to church with Chase's family. But how? She'd always attended when she lived here before, so his mom would surely invite her. Her best shot would be if this wasn't their week to go on the rotation schedule. That would buy her time.

Somehow, it just didn't seem right to go to church mad.

"There you are." Janice entered from the kitchen, fastening an earring in place. For a change, her short, highlighted hair wasn't covered by her food prep cap. "Why aren't you ready for church?"

Her hopes quickly dashed, Landry tried a different route. "Don't I need to get on the rotation schedule?"

"Nonsense. Come with us this week. Then we'll see about the timetable." Janice smoothed a hand down her stylish skirt.

"I don't want to take advantage."

Janice's knowing eyes saw straight through her. "Why don't you want to go? Come on. You can talk to me."

She'd been able to fake it in Aubrey—telling her family she was going with a friend in Denton. All the while, she'd left early on Sunday mornings, sat at the park until churches let out. Landry should have known that living and working in such close quarters, she'd never be able to get past Janice.

"Spill." Janice patted her hand.

"I haven't been to church since Kyle left me at the altar." There. She'd said it. Admitted the thing no one knew. Except God.

"Why?"

"Because I've been so mad." She hugged herself. "And bitter toward Kyle. I haven't felt like going."

"Ah, I see." Janice pulled up a tall stool and settled across the counter from her. "I remember how much you always loved church when you lived here with us."

"I adored everything about it. The hymns, the fellowship, the sermons."

"Don't you think this bitterness is hurting *you* instead of Kyle?" Janice patted her hand again and stood. "Think about that. I'd better light a fire under that man of mine or we'll be late." She hurried through the kitchen doors.

Such quiet wisdom. Landry missed church.

Missed God. She stood, rounded the counter and bolted for her private quarters.

"Whoa." Chase met her coming out of the office. "What's your hurry?"

At least she hadn't smacked into him this time. "I have to get ready for church."

"You're going?"

"If you'll stop talking and let me get ready."

"By all means." He stepped aside, ushered her on.

God would forgive her absence. Maybe He could help her sort out her muddled feelings for Chase.

Sunlight streamed through the stained glass windows splashing the walls of the hundred-year-old church with color. As the sermon wound down and the pastor made his altar plea to the congregation, Chase's mind wandered.

He'd invited Landry to come last week, but she'd worried about disrupting the rest of the staff's church attendance. Why wasn't she concerned about the rotation schedule now? Was she so distraught over Kyle's engagement, she needed God?

His mouth went dry.

Even if Kyle had driven her here, Chase was glad she'd come.

The piano started as a backdrop to the pastor's prayer, and several people went to the altar. Including Landry.

Chase followed, knelt by her side. After a silent

prayer for God to ease her hurt, Chase switched to his own needs. *Lord, if this can work out with Landry, pave a way for us to run the ranch together.* As his burden eased, he went down his usual list of prayers for his family and friends.

Landry stood before he did, went back to their pew. A minute or so later, he followed.

Over her head, he noticed his mom with a knowing grin on her face.

No doubt about it. Mom was on to him.

The music faded away, and a deacon closed the service with prayer.

Conversations began as the congregation scattered, and Chase turned to Landry.

"I'm glad you came."

"Me, too." Her smile went all the way to her eyes.

Something he hadn't seen enough of since she'd arrived at the ranch.

"You still got it?" The usual question from a gruff voice.

With a grin, Chase dug the knife from his pocket and turned around.

Dressed in his Sunday overalls, Wallace clapped Landry on the back solidly. Probably rattled her teeth. "She's a church girl. I told you she wasn't a scammer. You should go for her."

"Stop haranguing the young folks." Ms. Fay patted Landry's arm. "You'll have to forgive him.

He gets bored since he retired. I'm Fay, Wallace's wife." She offered her hand to Landry.

"Landry Malone."

"Ms. Fay was my Sunday school teacher." Chase gave her a hug. "My favorite one."

"I told you about her." Wallace pointed at her. "She's Chase's girlfriend."

"No!" Their voices blended.

"Business partner. Girlfriend." Wallace harrumphed. "What's the difference? If she's not your girlfriend now, she will be. I can tell when a young man's smitten."

"Stop it." Ms. Fay sent a chiding glare at her husband. "You're turning her downright purple. It was nice meeting you, Landry. We hope to see you again. Maybe next time, I'll duct tape his mouth first."

Landry chuckled. "It was nice meeting you, too."

As they made their way to the exit, a dozen more people stopped to introduce themselves to Landry. A few assumed she was Chase's girlfriend but accepted their joint protests.

"Landry, I'm so glad you're here." Jed limped toward them. "I brought something I was gonna send home with Chase for you." He dug in the shopping bag looped over his arm and pulled out a cedar box.

"For me?" Landry clasped a hand to her heart.

"It's sooo beautiful. But I couldn't. You could sell this."

"No." With a sad shake of his head, he turned the box around.

There was a gold plate with Eden's name engraved into it.

Chase's throat clogged.

"It's a jewelry box. Here, help me with it, Chase." He handed the box to Chase, opened the lid revealing little compartments and a removable tray. "I was making it for her wedding, but I didn't quite get it finished in time. And then... I couldn't possibly sell it, and I thought about giving it to Ms. Janice. But she doesn't wear much jewelry. I noticed you did."

Tears filled Landry's eyes, and she hurled herself at Jed. "I'll treasure it."

He turned beet-red, patted her back.

"I don't have anything of hers." Landry pulled away from him. "I mean, other than half a dude ranch, I guess." She swallowed hard. "I'm honored that you want me to have this gift meant for her. Especially after meeting me only once."

"Eden wouldn't have included you in her will if she didn't love you. If she didn't think you worthy."

"Thank you." Her chin trembled. "You have no idea what this means to me."

Jed ducked his head, squeezed her arm and turned toward the exit.

Landry swiped at her tears and reached for the

box as if Chase might keep it from her. He handed it over, and she ran her hand over the smooth wood, clutched it to her chest. Her love for his sister glowing in her glossy eyes.

"Let's go home," he said. It sounded good. Right. For them to share the dude ranch.

When he'd learned about Eden's will, he'd resented Landry and been suspicious of her motives. Now, within a week and a half of her arrival, he felt great respect for her.

Maybe a friendship with Landry could fill the empty space his sister had left in his life.

With the Monday morning breakfast rush over, Chase stepped into the kitchen. Mom and Dad busily sliced and diced. Most of his life had been spent looking at the tops of their puffy white shower caps.

But now they had a new addition. Pale red-gold tendrils curled out from beneath the pouf of Landry's hat. A distracting addition.

"I'm off to the fishmonger in San Antonio."

"Wow." Landry adjusted her apron straps. "I forgot all about our fish."

"Ron took them in. All processed and ready to get picked up."

"I haven't been to San Antonio since I finished school." Her tone held a lilt of nostalgia.

"Why don't you go with him?" Mom's perky tone strangled his last nerve. But she never looked up from her tomatoes. "Mondays are usually slow around here."

"I couldn't. I already left y'all in the lurch last week."

"We've got this." Dad whisked eggs in a huge bowl. "Go shopping or whatever young girls do these days."

"I'm not your typical shopper. I'm a flea market freak."

"Really?" Mom looked up at Chase, grinning from ear to ear. "Chase is, too. And there's one about ten minutes from the fish market."

"Resa did tell me she saw some cowhides at a steal there." Why had he admitted that? All he had to do was say he didn't have time. Had pressing things to get back to. "Maybe I could lasso a few for the ranch."

"Still." Landry nibbled her lip. "I hate to leave y'all shorthanded."

"Don't take this like we don't need you around here. You've been a great help to us." Mom started on an onion. "But we managed fine before you came. We can manage one more day without you."

"If you're sure." Landry wiped her hands on her apron. "I'll grab my purse. But this is the last time. At least for a week." She hurried out of the kitchen.

Chase waited until the door closed behind her. "I wish you'd stop forcing her on me," he whispered.

"Oh, pooh." Mom waved her latexed hand

through the air. "You both like to flea market. You'll have fun."

"The last time I tried to avoid a woman the way you're trying to shake Landry—" Dad shot him a wink "—I ended up marrying her."

"Think I'll wait in the foyer." Where it was quieter.

Moments later, Landry exited the great room, clutching her purse. With her apron and shower cap still on.

"You gonna wear that?"

She glanced down. "Oh." Color washed over her face as her hands went to her head. "Now I'll have hairnet hair, which is always so attractive." She pulled it and her apron off, stashed them in the kitchen.

Back in the foyer, she bent over at the waist, hanging her head upside down, and combed her fingers through her hair, stirring up a watermelon scent. When she tossed it back in place, his breath stopped.

"It looks bad, doesn't it?"

A mute shake of his head was all Chase could come up with.

"Oh, well." She shrugged.

Effortless, unconcerned, no fuss. Yet beauty that took his breath away.

"Let me load the coolers in the truck." Like a man headed for the gallows, he grabbed his keys.

* * *

Landry sat in the passenger seat of Chase's truck, wondering why he'd asked her to come along. He'd been standoffish with her since the start, but now he was okay with her company?

Now that she thought about it, though, Landry realized he hadn't really asked her. His mom had. So why had Landry been eager?

Because she'd never been to the fishmonger? Because she loved flea markets? Yes on both. But even more so because for some reason, she enjoyed spending time with him.

Why, when he didn't want her around? He'd eased up a bit, maybe even trusted her, and they'd had that bonding moment at church yesterday when Jed gave her the jewelry box. But they still weren't to the point of being friends.

"Have you ever been to the River Walk?" Chase merged expertly into traffic.

"Eden and I used to go there after our classes."

"What about the Alamo?"

"No."

"And they haven't stripped you of your Texas citizenship?"

She laughed. "I just never got around to it. Maybe we can do that next time." Now, why had she said that? He was only making conversation and obviously didn't want there to be a next time.

And to prove it, he didn't comment.

"Want to go our separate ways, call each other

when we're finished?" He eased into a parking lot, killed the engine.

"But if we're shopping for cowhides or anything else for the dude ranch—don't we need to agree on it?" Maybe they weren't friends, but they should make business decisions together.

"You're right. Sit tight—I'll get your door." He rounded the truck, opened her side and offered a hand as she climbed down. "Eden always gave me authority to make purchases for the ranch. But she knew me. Knew my taste."

Warmth spread through her as he kept her hand in his. Her gaze met his. He cleared his throat and let go of her. "Better get to shopping."

Do not fall for him, she warned her heart.

He strode toward a huge metal building. "Resa said the cowhides are in the second aisle."

She tried to match his pace, but since three of her steps made up one of his, she practically ran to catch up.

"Sorry." He slowed. "Eden always said she had to gallop to keep up with me."

"I'll bet. Her legs were shorter than mine." She eased up, relaxed a bit.

He opened the door for her, and they stepped inside the air-conditioned warehouse. Aisles lined the concrete. There was a stale smell of used furniture, old books and dust. But the market was neat and organized.

"There they are." He cut down the second aisle, examined a cowhide.

"These are really nice."

"And about a hundred dollars less than the usual price you find. Let's get two. If that's okay with you?"

"Just a curious question. What do we do with them at the dude ranch?"

He grinned. "Walk on them."

"That seems like such a shame." She ran her hand over the smooth hide. "Doesn't it wear them out?"

"Eventually. But then we get new ones."

"We could hang them on the wall. Then they'd stay nice."

"They're rugs."

"Or wall hangings."

"Tell you what." His sigh echoed exasperation. "We'll get one for a rug and one for a wall hanging."

"Deal."

He reached for a black-and-white one.

"Wait." She set her hand on his arm but quickly withdrew when she felt his muscles beneath her fingers. "Where will they go?"

"This one for the Cattle Baron Room, and another for the foyer."

"I remember rugs in both places."

"Several long-term guests have missed them. I've been keeping my eye out for a good deal."

"So these will get trampled to death. Especially the one in the foyer."

He closed his eyes. "It's. A. Rug."

"Since you like the black-and-white and there are no other hides in the lobby, it can go there. But we should hang it on the side of the staircase and get a less expensive rug for the floor. Maybe from Resa."

"As much as I hate to admit it—" his gaze narrowed "—that actually makes sense."

"See? We might can get the hang of this compromise thing." As long as her heart didn't get compromised in the process. "The Cattle Baron Room has a brown-and-white bedspread." She tapped her chin with her finger. "Doesn't it?"

"I reckon we should stick with that color scheme?" He pulled a sour face as if he'd just lost his man card by discussing such things.

She flipped through the hides, found a nice brown-and-white one with lots of splotches. "What about this one?"

"I'll take them to the front so nobody nabs them." He tugged the two hides they'd chosen down, folded them into a bundle as if the heavy skins weighed nothing and carried them to the register.

Landry scanned the surrounding booths. A cameo necklace caught her eye. Peach and white, delicately carved with a filigree chain. Her breath stalled as she picked up the piece.

"Find something?"

"It reminds me of the one your grandmother used to wear."

"Me, too. How much is it?"

She turned it over. "Twenty-three ninety-five."

"Costume at that price."

"Granny's was, too. Your gramps got it for her…"

"Early in their marriage." For once he didn't seem annoyed that she knew so much about his family.

They strolled the rest of the booths, and Landry found a handmade Victorian-style quilt sewn in a lovely yellow rose fabric. "This will look great on Granny's bed."

"Your bed." Resignation sounded in Chase's tone. That Granny was gone? Or that he was stuck with Landry?

They agreed on a wagon wheel wall hanging for the Desperado Room and took their purchases to the register. After Landry paid for her personal items, the clerk slid her necklace into a small sack.

"I'll take that." Chase picked up all their bags along with the hides.

"I can carry something."

"I've got it."

She followed him out and hurried ahead to open the back door of his dual cab pickup.

Chase set the hides and the bag with her quilt in the seat.

"My necklace?"

"Let me." He pulled the tiny sack from his pocket. "Hold your hair up."

"I don't have to wear it now." Her hand went to her throat.

"I want to see how it looks."

She turned her back to him.

"At least, I *think* I can latch it," he said. The pendant dropped in front of her face, his massive hands holding each end of the fragile chain. "Don't know why they make such tiny little clasps."

"They're made for women." She pulled her hair up for him.

"Then why do women always have their men fasten their necklaces for them?" His hand grazed her neck.

Shivers went through her. But he was not her man.

"Because we can't see what we're doing." He could not be her man. She would never allow herself to fall for another man.

"There. Let me see." His hands moved away.

The pendant fell heavy at the hollow of her collarbone. She turned to face him.

"I'll tell you one thing." His gaze met hers, then dropped to the cameo. "You're not anybody's granny."

"Thanks." Her face heated, and she scurried to the passenger side, eager to get to the fish market, then back to the dude ranch and escape this one-on-one time with him.

"You hungry?" Chase beat her to it and opened her door for her.

"A little." She climbed in. "We could drive through and get something."

"I'd rather find somewhere to eat in." He rounded the truck, slid in and started the engine. "How about the Tower of the Americas? Ever been?"

"That's the glass restaurant that rotates, right?" The one stuck way up in the sky? Just the thought of it set her nerves on edge.

"Seven hundred fifty feet up. Within an hour's time, you get a bird's-eye view of the entire city. You can sit back and enjoy a five-star meal that you didn't have to cook."

"Never been." Her throat constricted. "I was on a budget in culinary school. If our creations in class were edible, we ate there." She giggled, trying to squelch the fear coiling in her stomach. "Am I dressed nice enough?" She glanced down at her turquoise top paired with white capris and heeled silver sandals.

"There will be people dolled up and some wearing jeans. There's no dress code."

Her hair was an unruly tangle, but her clothes were probably appropriate. She was just searching for an excuse not to go.

"I'm game." Why had she agreed? All she had to do was say she was tired, that they should head back.

But if this was another one of his tests, she refused to fail it.

"You'd think it wouldn't be this busy on a Monday afternoon." Chase tapped his foot while they waited for an elevator. "Seems like most folks would be at work."

"Maybe we should do this another time, since we already got the fish."

"Those are commercial-grade coolers. They'd be fine in there for two days."

"Are you sure? We probably should have picked them up last."

"Positive." Was she in that much of a rush to get away from him? "I'll tell you what I'm not having—fish. In fact after seeing that bucket of heads, if I wasn't an avid fish lover, I'd never eat it again."

"It was fascinating." Her words tumbled out with excitement. "They were so fast with the knives and fish flying. It was fun. Surely, you've cleaned your own."

"Yes. But not that many at one time. I've never smelled so much slime or seen more guts…" He made a gagging sound. "I may have nightmares."

"What's wrong, tough guy?"

He grimaced. "Something smelled fishy in there. My sinuses won't recover for a week."

"But you've been there before."

"Not where the action is."

"If it would fit FDA standards, I'd have done it myself."

"I don't believe I've ever met anyone quite like you, Landry Malone."

"Because I don't mind fish slime?"

"And you still look like a girl." He chuckled.

The elevator doors opened, and they waited as people exited. More rushed in around them. As they stepped inside, Landry slipped her hand into his. Odd.

"You okay?" he whispered.

"Just a little motion sickness."

"Why didn't you tell me?"

"How else would we get up?" The doors shut and the car slowly ascended. Her face blanched. "It's just that my stomach is still at the bottom."

But as they climbed the tower, she squeezed tighter. By the time they made it to the top, she had a death grip on him, with his fingers on the verge of tingling.

"Let me guess. You're afraid of heights?"

"A little," she squeaked, sucked in a big breath. "But I refuse to be ruled by my fears."

"You should have said something. We can eat at another restaurant. On ground level."

"No. I'm fine."

The doors opened, and he ushered her out. She

was still wobbly, so he tucked her hand in the crook of his arm.

She bobbled despite his support.

"Whoa." Chase gripped her elbow to steady her. "Let's go someplace else."

"I've heard it's good here. And I'm hungry." She straightened her spine.

"Listen, you've proven your point." Amazingly, she didn't protest as he turned her back to the elevator. "You're tough as nails. But I won't keep you here, expect you to eat, when you're positively green."

She leaned into him.

"I'm sorry, Landry." He nestled her against his side. "I'll get you down, and I'll never take you anywhere like this again."

"You promise?" Her voice quivered.

"Promise." He pushed the button. But with every minute that passed, she became more jittery. "We're almost out of here."

"Let the record show—this is the only test I've failed."

"But I wasn't testing you. I had no idea."

The elevator dinged and the doors opened.

"Landry?" said a preppy guy in a skinny suit.

Kyle Billings. With his new fiancée on his arm.

Chase recognized him from Googling Landry along with her internet search history.

Was that regret in Kyle's eyes? Did he want her

back? He should have regrets—the heel. He was unworthy of Landry.

But why did Chase care?

"Hello, Kyle." Landry's face was stricken. And Chase didn't know if there was anything he could do to protect her.

Chapter Seven

Landry concentrated on schooling her features. She couldn't give away that she was affected in any way by seeing the man she'd planned to marry for the first time since he left her at the altar in the midst of their vows. Or that the curvy blonde draped on his arm bothered her in the slightest.

"You two know each other?" The blonde looked down her perfect nose at Landry—even though they were about the same height.

"Kyle left Landry at the altar last year." Sarcasm rolled off Chase's tongue, malice in the glare he aimed at Kyle.

Landry closed her eyes. "Chase."

"You were engaged before?" The blonde turned on Kyle.

"I'm sorry, Waverly." Kyle ran his hand along the back of his neck. "It didn't seem important enough to tell you."

Landry's face scalded. His careless words like a kick in the stomach.

"But she's *so* not your type." Waverly sneered.

Why hadn't she worn something nicer? Compared to the blonde's skintight white dress, Landry felt tomboyish, dowdy and faded.

"Maybe not, but she's so my type." Chase's arms came around her waist and hauled her back against him as he buried his face in her hair.

"What are you…?" She struggled against him.

"Come on, sweetheart. Don't be shy." Chase chuckled against her ear. "Kyle knows exactly how hard it is to resist your fiery locks. No need to hide that I'm crazy in love with you."

His warm breath sent a shiver over her. Pretending. To save her embarrassment. She stopped fighting him, but he must have felt the heat coming off her face.

Kyle's gaze locked on hers. "I'm glad you've moved on, that you have someone. It makes me feel better about—things." He gave her a tight smile. "Be happy, Landry."

"I've lost my appetite." Waverly jerked away from him and bolted into the elevator. Kyle followed, barely making it inside before the doors started closing.

"I can't believe you never told me—" Waverly's tirade cut short as the doors shut.

But with Kyle gone, Chase didn't let Landry go. His warm breath stirred the hair at her temple, sending another shiver over her. He was pretending. So why did the embrace feel so real? So right?

"My hair isn't fiery. It's strawberry blond," she

said after she started breathing again, jabbing her elbow into his ribs.

"Ouch." He let go of her.

"What was that about?" She spun away from him.

"It was either punch him or take up for you. And I figured I'd get us kicked out if I punched him."

"Exactly how is lying about our relationship taking up for me?"

"Yeah, sorry about that." He clenched his fists. "I had to do something to stop that witch's gloating, and I wanted to spare you embarrassment."

"I appreciate your concern." She pressed her hands to each temple, willing her brain not to blow up. "But I'm a big girl."

"Maybe thinking we're an item will torment him."

"I doubt he'll spare a thought for me." Not with his new fiancée to keep him company.

But Chase had only tried to help. Misguided as his methods might have been.

"Thank you for trying to help." She clasped a hand to her heart. Did she sound normal? She was too affected to tell. "It was just a shock. To see him again. With her." Kyle had obviously moved on with no problem. Maybe he hadn't loved her, either. Or maybe he'd dumped her for this Waverly person.

And it was no wonder. There was no way Landry could measure up.

She winced. "Why does she have to be so supermodel worthy?"

"Some guys are more into the athletic, strawberry blond, with freckles sprinkled across her nose type." He waggled his eyebrows at her.

And her face went hot. Yeah, right. "Thanks. But you're not making me feel any better."

"Comparing Waverly to you is like the contrast between a peacock and a swan. Some men fall for the prideful strutting of the overembellished peacock. But some prefer the grace and simple beauty of a swan. After almost landing you, ending up with Waverly would be a letdown."

"Thanks." Her laugh came out shaky. "I'm really fine. More mad than upset. How did you even know who he was?"

"I might have—sort of checked your search history that night you got so upset." He grimaced. "Not my finest moment, but I was worried. I put two and two together from things Mom told me."

So he knew all about the most humiliating skeletons in her closet. Her face went hotter.

She turned to the window. Remembering where they were. In a thimble perched in the sky on a toothpick. Her stomach clenched and her head whirled.

"Lean on me." He put his arm around her waist, gently leading her away from the glass. "Let's get you down from here."

They walked back to the elevator, but for once, her fear of heights was the least of her problems. Why was Chase's kindness stirring up more inside her than seeing Kyle had?

They strolled to the ranch house side by side. Why did it feel so right? His presence made her feel safe.

"Want to sit a spell? Let the frog chorus cure what ails you?" He stopped on the porch.

She sank into the swing. For now, just for this moment in time, she couldn't pull herself away from Chase.

Especially since he'd been so sweet today. Perfectly content to drive through Whataburger. Comfort food in the parking lot instead of the nice, sit down meal he'd intended.

"I don't know what you ever saw in Mr. Preppy Frat Boy." He settled beside her. "I mean, he wears skinny suits."

"Not my favorite look." She wrinkled her nose. "He was so different from the ranch hands I was used to." But she hadn't loved him. What if he hadn't walked out on her? What if she hadn't realized she didn't love him until they'd said their I do's?

"He probably doesn't even own a pair of jeans, and if he does, they're probably skinny, too. With cuffs." He lowered his voice in a conspiratorial manner. "Never trust a man who rolls up his denim. And especially never trust a man who doesn't wear it at all."

"Wish I'd known that last year." She giggled as her eyes met his. "She deserves him. Who names a child Waverly, anyway? Makes me think of fabric."

"Sorry. I didn't get that reference. I'm afraid I'm not a fabric aficionado."

But to her horror, her laugh ended in a hiccupped sob.

He traced the moisture down her cheek with a gentle thumb.

"I always cry when I'm mad," she huffed. "And it only makes me madder."

"Kyle has no idea what he missed out on." He pulled her into his arms.

She should have pulled away. But she didn't have the strength to. She had too many feelings stuffed inside to contain. Anger at Kyle. Confusion that she actually thought she'd loved him. Disappointment that she couldn't trust her own heart now that she'd met a really great guy.

She shuddered against Chase, struggled to get her emotions under control. But the dam inside her burst. She soaked his shoulder but at least managed to silence the sobs pushing to the surface.

He didn't say anything, just held her.

She felt one of the barriers between them slip away.

With her tears subsiding, she should move

away from him. But she wasn't a pretty crier. Her makeup was waterproof, but her sensitive skin wasn't.

And his embrace seemed to give her strength. She just wanted to eke out a little more time with him. A bit more of this newly discovered closeness between them.

"That thing you said about me testing you—I had no idea you were afraid of heights. I wouldn't have taken you there if I had. You must think I'm a complete jerk."

"You have to admit you were pretty rough on me that first week."

"Let's just say I've run into a few untrustworthy women in my time. Women willing to do anything to—"

"Get the dude ranch. I know."

"Who told you?" He stiffened. "Mom? Resa?"

"No. I won't reveal my source. The person who told me was only trying to help me understand why you were being such an ogre."

"Ogre, huh?" He relaxed again with a chuckle. "Well, I apologize. No more tests. No more orneriness. Maybe we could call a truce. Try that friend thing you mentioned. And honor Eden's memory."

"I like that idea. A lot."

The back door opened. "Landry?" His mom stepped out on the porch. "Oh, dear, are you all right?"

She pulled away from him and dabbed her eyes. "I was just lending a much-needed shoulder." Chase patted her arm.

His mom leaned in the doorway, green eyes scrutinizing them.

"I'm fine." Landry tried to collect herself. It couldn't get any worse. "Chase has a great shoulder." Oh, but it could. If only biting her tongue in two would retrieve what she'd just said.

A smile tugged at his mom's mouth. "Y'all are getting quite cozy."

"Mom!"

At least Landry's face was probably red enough now to blend the blotches together. "It's not like that. I'm just having a bad day. Chase was only offering comfort."

"From enemies to comfort within two weeks' time. Wonder what next week will bring?"

"All right." Chase stood, linked arms with his mom and propelled her inside. "You've mortified Landry enough."

"I'm sorry. I didn't mean to embarrass anyone. I just—" The kitchen door closed behind them.

But Janice had a valid point. Things were way too cozy.

Today Landry had run into the man she'd almost married, realized for certain she'd never loved him and had been smacked in the face with her replacement.

Yet all she could think about was Chase.

* * *

Chase stashed his tools back in the maintenance closet. He'd managed to stay busy and avoid Mom's questions about yesterday with Landry. But this evening as he headed for the door, he found his mother waiting on the front porch.

"Did you need something?"

"I thought we'd talk for a sec."

He had a trail ride to guide in a few minutes. And he'd hoped to get away without running into anyone. He loved his mom, but he was too confused to discuss Landry.

"I have only a few to spare." He settled in the log chair, gestured her to the one beside it.

"You have feelings for Landry."

Deny it or admit it? Which would end the conversation? Probably neither.

A breeze whispered through the live oaks overhead. What was it about Landry? Why did she draw him like moth to a bug zapper?

"Hello?"

"It's complicated." He clamped his back teeth together, hoping she'd let the subject drop.

"What's complicated about it? I think you're convinced now she's not a scammer." She shot him a knowing grin. "You're both Christians, unattached, perfect for each other."

"No." He shook his head. "It can't happen."

"Why not?"

"She's still hung up on Kyle."

"You really think so? After the way he hurt her, not to mention humiliated the poor child to the point that she felt she had to move away from everything and everyone she knew?"

"We ran into him and his fiancée yesterday." He scrubbed a hand across the stubble of his beard. "I saw what it did to her. Caught the tears."

"Kyle is engaged? Already?" Mom gave a dismissive wave of her hand. "Well, that just means he's effectively out of Landry's picture. Maybe you can help her forget him."

"No way am I going there." His gaze went to the puffy white clouds overhead. "Rebound relationships usually don't last. And we own a business together. Getting involved with Landry would only complicate everything. Especially if it didn't work out."

"But if it did work out, y'all could run this place together and live happily ever after."

"Mom." Chase stood. "No more talking. Please."

She made a zipper motion across her mouth and headed inside.

As the door shut behind her, Levi ambled up the path from the barn.

"Hey, boss." His words were thick and slurred together, the *s* sounding like *th*.

"Are you drunk?" Please, no. Levi was invaluable to the ranch as a hand and trail guide, but their strict no-booze policy applied to everyone.

"You know I don't drink. I had a root canal this morning. Just woke up."

Chase winced. "Sorry for the assumption. But I don't think you're up for our ride."

"Feeling no pain. Good drugs." Levi waggled his eyebrows. "Doc said I'm good to go."

In his right mind, Levi was the epitome of responsible and reliable. But tonight, not so much.

It was the Sanchezes' last night here. He couldn't cancel the trail ride and camping trip on them. But he couldn't depend on Levi in this condition.

"How about you go sleep it off? I'll get someone else."

"But really, I'm okay." The more the man talked, the more drunk he sounded. "Except for operating heavy machinery."

"I'm thinking that might apply to a horse, too. I got this, buddy. Go rest." Chase clapped him on the back. "I'll get one of the other guys to drive you home."

"All righty then." Levi swayed.

"In fact." Chase grabbed his arm, led him to a chair. "Let's get you a seat."

"I'm fine." Levi sank down.

With him settled, Chase made the call, waited until one of the other hands headed from the barn.

Levi slumped in the chair, already snoring.

"I don't know how you were upright a few minutes ago." Chase chuckled.

"I got him," the other hand waved.

"Thanks." Chase stepped inside, cut through to the kitchen.

Mom chopped bell peppers while Dad and Landry rubbed seasoning into roasts lining the counter. Landry dropped hers into the pan, then looked up.

"Hey, Dad, any chance of you helping me with a trail ride? Levi ended up on the losing end of a dentist's drill, and he's on pain medication. With as many kids as I've got, I need two guides."

"Your father is a lot of things." Mom patted Dad on the shoulder. "Trail guide isn't one of them."

"The last time I tried riding for that long, I couldn't walk for days." Dad chuckled. "But Landry used to head them up when she lived here before."

Another surprise. An unwelcome one. He did not need to spend more time with Landry. With all his truce and friend talk, he wasn't sure he could pull that off. Not without wanting more from her.

If only she were unqualified for their new guidelines. But he already knew she was certified in CPR.

"I'm preparing for tomorrow's lunch." Landry's gaze skittered back to her roast.

"We've got this." Mom started on another pepper, her knife making rhythmic slices. "Most of our guests are going on the ride, and we already packed their picnic supper. You've done the biggest prep for tomorrow by getting the roasts cooking. Go get ready while Chase gears the horses up."

"I guess I'll go put my boots on then." She washed her hands, exited the kitchen.

Chase shot his mom a look.

"What?" She gave him an innocent shrug. But her grin oozed pure cunning.

He hurried out to the barn, where the ranch hands had the horses ready. Their guests who'd signed up for the ride circled the livestock. He really needed to get the ranch hands trained in CPR so he wouldn't have to take Landry along again.

By the time she strolled their way, they'd managed to get everyone mounted. They formed a half circle around him with his bay and the one he'd chosen for Landry, a palomino.

"This is Pearl." He stroked the creamy horse's neck, the animal's platinum tail swishing. "She's gentle and easy to handle."

"I know my way around a horse." She lowered her voice. "But I'm surprised you didn't give me a stallion."

His mouth twitched. "Wish I'd thought of that your first week here."

Her eyes narrowed, but there was teasing in their depths. "She's exquisite." She turned to the horse, smoothed her hand over Pearl's velvety snout, then set her foot in the stirrup.

"She is." He hurried to help, but she swung up into her saddle before he could get there.

"Good girl." She patted the horse's shoulder.

"Everyone ready?" He mounted his horse.

The kids' eager shouts echoed through the air.

"I'll take the lead. You bring up the rear. Make sure no one strays." Chase clicked his tongue, and his bay sauntered toward the trail, its russet coat gleaming in the waning sun, black mane swaying with the movement of its massive shoulders.

Excited voices, the clop of hooves and chatter filled the woods as they headed down the trail he knew like the freckles scattered over Landry's nose he'd recently memorized.

Somehow over the last week, despite his best efforts, he'd started needing her near. Needing her as much as he needed pure Texas air to breathe.

Twisted, gnarled live oaks lined each side. Mexican hat wildflowers scattered about with their cones in the middle and droopy yellow petals. White rocks and cypress lined the river. He usually gave a running commentary, pointing out everything to their guests, but he just couldn't focus.

As they neared the fence separating their property from Resa McCall's, his gut sank. Telltale brown leaves on at least three live oaks.

And suddenly his problems were way bigger than Landry. Because he wasn't sure they could afford a bout of the oak wilt fungus he was seeing on those leaves. He knew this newly formed partnership with Landry would be going through another test. If they didn't take care of the problem quickly, it could effectively shut down the ranch.

The fire pit cast a glow on each face in the circle as the logs popped and hissed. Too warm for a fire, but no one seemed to mind. They just scooted their chairs back. Night sounds filled the air— the vibrating buzz of cicadas mixed with crickets chirping, frogs croaking and the occasional hoot from an owl.

Chase had been unusually quiet during the trail ride. Back when Landry had led them, she'd done a running narrative on the types of trees, the horses and even the weeds—which she was actually allergic to. If not for the allergy pill she took daily, the frothy, lacy milkweed and the vibrant orange butterfly weed would send her into a sneezing frenzy.

Maria finished her s'more, then skipped— braids bouncing—around the seated adults and stopped beside her mom, who uncrossed her legs and helped Maria onto her lap.

As the other kids and several adults finished their s'mores, the mom stroked her daughter's braid. "I used to wear a braid when I was little. Grandma used to fix my hair for me."

"Really?" Maria turned sideways and looked up at her. "I wanna be beautiful like you when I grow up, Mommy."

Maria's mom hugged her, sticky fingers, grass-stained knees and all. "You're already beautiful, sweetie."

Tenderness and love glowed out of Maria's dad as he watched his wife. That was what real love looked like.

Kyle had never looked at Landry like that. And she'd never looked at him that way, either.

They'd been a train wreck waiting to happen. Him trying to change her, her trying to force her happily-ever-after. She'd used him to make her dreams come true. She was as much at fault as he was.

But he had to have known before the wedding that he didn't want to go through with it. All he'd had to do was tell her. Instead he'd embarrassed her in front of practically everyone she knew.

Yet Jesus had gone through so much more. Tortured and dying on a cross, all the while asking his father to forgive his tormentors.

Her heart twisted. Since attending church again, she'd prayed for God to help her forgive Kyle. *I'm sorry for being bitter, Lord.* A heavy burden lifted. *I forgive Kyle.*

That odd sensation crept up the back of her neck, like someone was staring at her. She scanned the circle. Chase.

But the corners of his mouth tipped down, a sadness in his eyes. Was he thinking about Eden? His sister had always enjoyed sitting around the fire pit. Though she never camped out, she loved when they were brimming with guests. Especially kids. Even though almost ten months had passed, it was still hard to fathom she was gone.

He averted his gaze. "Who all wants to camp out tonight?"

"Me. Me. Me," excited children echoed.

The parents had planned the surprise for the kids, but the grandparents were going back to the ranch house.

"Okay." Chase brushed his hands off and stood. "I set up five tents earlier. Each couple will have their own tent, the girls get one, the boys another, I have one and I can set one up in case you wanted to stay, Landry."

"I'm in." She loved camping. And in spite of herself, she loved being near Chase.

Something raced over his expression too fast for her to read. Pleasure. Disappointment. A mixture. She wasn't sure. Did he regret letting that barrier slip away?

"I have wet wipes for messy hands and faces." She passed out several containers.

"Exactly what we need." The moms eagerly swabbed their kids despite their protests.

One of the Sanchez dads rose to his feet. "Let's hit our sleeping bags, then."

"Aww. Not yet," one of the kids protested.

"The fire's dying down, and Mr. Chase needs

to put it out so he can turn in." The youngest mom looked toward the sky with a dramatic eye roll. "Besides, y'all will be up at the crack of dawn."

The two couples stood, and the kids reluctantly trailed to their tents.

The Sanchez patriarch heaved himself up, assisted his wife. "Don't we need to help with the mess?"

"I'll get it." Chase picked up a few paper plates and cups, tossed them into the fire. With a whoosh, they turned to ash. "Landry will take y'all back to the ranch house." He started folding empty chairs and blankets. "I'll call the hands, so they'll meet you to take care of the horses."

"I'll be back." She swung up in her saddle while he helped the elder Sanchezes.

Ideally when she returned, he'd still be sitting at the fire. And she could join him. For what?

She should go back to the ranch house and stay there. Call Chase and tell him she'd changed her mind about camping.

"See if Mom and Dad can come with you. Not to camp—unless they want to. But I need to talk to them."

"Okay." So much for spending time alone. Probably for the best. She trotted her horse into the darkness.

The Sanchez grandparents followed.

Something was wrong. Chase had been so quiet—none of his usual clowning to entertain their guests. So distracted and serious. What could be bothering him just when they were starting to get along?

Chapter Eight

Hoofbeats echoed through the darkness. Landry emerged from the shadows into the well-lit campground first—her hair a tangled mass of curls, her cheeks flushed, his parents trailing behind.

All three dismounted, and Landry plopped on the blanket beside him.

Her knee brushed his as she curled her legs to the side away from him, her shoulder a breath away from his. His heart skipped a beat, his nerve endings on high alert.

His parents settled across from them. They were like two couples.

"I'm glad y'all could come." Chase turned to Landry, then wished he hadn't. He lowered his voice so their guests wouldn't overhear. "Did you see the trees by the fence on the McCall side?"

She squinted one eye—a gesture he recognized she did when she was thinking. "Not really."

"We've got oak wilt." He ran a hand through his hair. "At least three trees."

"Oh, no." Mom groaned.

Dad let out a heavily burdened sigh. "Ah, son. I'm sorry."

"Like that patch of dead trees down the road with the gray furry stuff on them?" Landry pointed west.

"That's oak wilt." Chase hung his head. "It starts with brown leaves, then the furry stuff, and the tree dies."

"That's so sad. That strip of trees used to be so pretty."

"This could be the end of the dude ranch."

"Why? So we lose some trees. Sad, but not the end of the world."

"It won't stop with three, Landry." All moisture evaporated from Chase's mouth. "It'll keep going until they're all dead. People come to dude ranches to go on trail rides, to camp, to have bonfires. In the woods."

Dad winced. "A friend from church had an outbreak last year. He lost most of his trees, and his neighbor lost some, too."

"But there's got to be some fungus killer we can spray. Right?"

"There is." Dad grabbed a stick, poked around in the fire. "But the most effective treatment is to have trenches dug to break up the root system and separate the diseased trees from the healthy ones. That's what he did, but it was almost too late."

"There you go." Landry splayed her hands. "We've got shovels."

"Four-foot-deep trenches." Chase met her gaze. Her smile faded. "We have a tractor."

"It takes more than a tractor. It's expensive." The glow of the fire highlighted the planes of Dad's face, the silver in his hair.

"How expensive?"

"When our friend reported his infestation, the company said usually two to eight thousand. His was so bad, he ended up paying much more." The graveness in Dad's tone sank something hard into the pit of Chase's stomach.

He saw Landry's mouth move, but nothing came out.

"Let's just pray it's not bad." Chase stood, paced around the fire.

"We could help shoulder the cost." Dad's eyebrows rose.

"No." Chase reclaimed his seat. "Y'all have your own business to worry about. I only told y'all because I remember you mentioning somebody who'd dealt with it."

"But we're in this together, son. What affects the dude ranch affects the restaurant."

"What do we do?" Landry's voice went an octave too high.

"We can try fungicide treatment. It's not nearly as effective but costs considerably less at one fifty per treatment."

"We'll do whatever it takes. If it's a bad outbreak, worst-case scenario—" Chase's breath caught in his lungs "—we'll get a loan." With business so spotty during the off-season, the last thing they needed was a big dent in the ranch account or to take on debt.

"Now, hold on, son. We may only be talking a few trees." Dad met his gaze across the fire. "We need to call the Texas A&M Forest Service. There's federal funding for this sort of thing that might help with the cost. And since it's near the fence, you need to contact Resa. It might affect her trees, as well, and maybe the McCalls could share the fees."

"They're rich." Landry's lips found a smile once more.

"We can't expect her to foot the bill." Chase scowled. "She already cut us a great deal when we updated our furnishings last year."

"Of course not. I just meant that she can afford her share—if her trees are affected. And maybe the forest services will aid us."

"Landry's right." Mom stood. "We might be stressing over nothing. And no matter what Chase says, we'll pay our share. If we lose dude ranch customers, we won't have anybody to feed in the restaurant. In the meantime, I say we enjoy the rest of the evening and make the call in the morning."

But Chase's anxiety didn't lift. What if there were more diseased trees scattered throughout the property? What if the oak wilt wasn't only in the beginning stages?

"Until then, stop worrying about it." Landry set her hand on his arm, sending his pulse into overdrive. "We'll figure it out."

"I'll try." He stood. "Stand back while I put the fire out."

His parents said their good-nights, mounted up and rode off into the shadows. Landry headed for her tent as he doused the fire with the water hose hooked to an old well Gramps had dug for safety purposes.

Wished he could douse his apprehension as easily.

Chase waved beside Landry until the two minivans full of Sanchezes drove out of sight.

"I'll miss them." She hugged herself.

"They're good folk. They seemed to have a really good time and mentioned coming back, so maybe we'll see them again." He gave her shoulder a squeeze, and saw her immediately wince.

"You okay?" He jerked his hand away.

"Just sore." With a sheepish grin, she massaged the side of her neck. "I haven't slept on the ground since… I don't even remember when. I didn't think I was gonna be able to move when I woke up this morning. What did the forestry service say?"

"Funding is in place for our area for cost sharing. They'll come for an inspection tomorrow."

"That's fast." She headed for the kitchen.

"Oak wilt doesn't rest." He followed.

His parents stood at the counter, Dad busily chopping and dicing while Mom flattened a mound of dough.

"Is Levi back at work today?" Mom's rolling pin was so quick, it seemed self-propelled.

"His jaw is the size of a boulder, but he says he's fine."

Landry grabbed her apron and food prep hat.

But Mom held her hands up. "You won't be needing those today."

"I won't?" Landry's movements stalled.

"I want Chase to go to The Apple Café in Medina and pick up the cases of preserves I ordered. And you're going with him."

His gaze swung to his mother's, but she ignored him.

"Don't I need to stay here and help?" Landry asked.

"I can handle the order myself." Chase's protest battled with Landry's. Obviously neither of them was into one-on-one time with each other.

"You have to experience The Apple Café." Mom clapped her hands, and a puff of flour formed a cloud in the air. "*Texas Monthly* listed it in the Top 40 Best Small Town Restaurants in Texas. You just can't beat the ambiance, and the food is wonderful. Might as well grab lunch while you're there. And have apple ice cream, then shop for preserves and the best sweet nut bread in Texas."

"You had me at apple ice cream. I remember

Granny trying to get me to go when I lived here before, but I was always studying." Landry put her apron and cap back on the hook. "But one of these days, y'all are gonna have to let me work."

"You earn your keep handling reservations, sharing your marketing skills and keeping the website up to date for the dude ranch. That you're a chef is just a nice bonus. But be sure and get back by church time tonight."

Great. How could he avoid Landry when his mom kept saddling him with her?

The Apple Café, the quaint eatery in Medina, fifteen minutes away from the dude ranch, was like nowhere Landry had ever been.

As Chase ushered her into line, she scanned the gravel floor and galvanized tin ceiling. "It has a charm all its own."

A scream erupted behind them.

Chase shielded Landry as a little girl did a wild, panicked dance, her hands flailing around her head.

"It's gone, punkin." A man scooped the child up. "Calm down. You're okay."

"Are you sure it's gone?" she whimpered, her face pressed into the man's chest as he walked away, comforting her.

Chase pointed to a sign.

Landry scanned it. Bee Careful! A warning and

pun in one, alerting customers to watch for honey bees. "So they let them hang out in the store."

"They have a hive outside and sell fresh honey here. They won't hurt you unless you mash them." Chase grinned. "Which can happen real easy if you dance around, waving your arms. The best thing to do is just be still until they go away."

"What can I get you, ma'am?" the clerk asked.

"Landry!" exclaimed a child's excited voice.

She turned in time to catch her former boss's daughter as she hurled herself at Landry. "Kayla? What are you doing here?"

"We're visiting Grandpa Warren. Mama said we'd come see you while we're here."

"I think you've gotten taller since I left."

Kayla beamed. "I'm almost—"

"Seven. I started working for your folks right after you were born, Munchkin."

"Didn't this work out well?" Rayna approached, followed by Clay.

"Rayna. It's so good to see y'all." Landry hugged her, then Clay, remembered Chase. "Chase, meet Rayna and Clay Warren, my former bosses. And their daughter, Kayla."

"Clay Warren." Chase's jaw dropped. "As in four-time World Champion Bull Rider Clay Warren?"

"That was a few moons ago." Clay ducked his head. Always humble.

Chase turned to Landry. "Why did you never

mention the dude ranch you worked for in Aubrey belonged to Clay Warren?"

"She never did pay me no mind." Clay shot her a wink.

"This is Chase Donovan, my business partner." She squelched a giggle as Chase did his level best to play it casual. Slack-jawed, shifting his weight back and forth. So unlike his usual calm, cool and collected self.

Rayna sized him up. "You two seem cozy."

"You'll have to forgive my wife." Clay put his arm around her. "Once she landed me, she turned into Miss Matchmaker."

Landry's cheeks flushed. "Chase and I have struck up a friendship." Is that what it was?

"Eat lunch with us, Landry." Kayla bounced up and down. "Please. Please. Please."

"Do you mind, Chase?"

"Lunch with Clay Warren?" His grin widened. "I think I can manage."

"I'm buying." Clay clapped him on the back.

"Now, that's not necessary."

"You're coming to Ally's wedding." Rayna linked arms with Landry. "Right?"

"I wouldn't miss it." But her tone fell flat, even though she'd tried to sound excited.

She loved her cousin, was happy for her, but weddings left a bad taste in her mouth these days. Especially one in her hometown. Especially after seeing Kyle again.

But even more worrisome than the wedding, she could tell by the way Rayna was scrutinizing them, she wasn't buying that they were only friends. By tomorrow morning, it would be all over Aubrey that Landry had a new boyfriend.

A rumor would convince everyone she'd moved on. But it wasn't true. And come time for Ally's wedding, she'd show up alone. And everyone would feel sorry for her all over again.

Chase opened the truck door for Landry. "I still can't believe you never mentioned who your former boss was." He'd read where she worked when he'd Googled her. But hadn't put it together.

"To me, he's just Clay." She shrugged as she strolled toward the ranch house.

"So, who's Ally, and why don't you want to go to her wedding?"

"She's my cousin, and I do want to go. It's just that…"

"What?" He settled on the porch swing, patted the seat beside him.

"There I was." Her sigh resonated from the top of her head to her polished toenails as she settled beside him. "On the brink of what I thought would be my happily-ever-after." She closed her eyes as if she could see it all playing out again. "Kyle was in the middle of his vows when he just stopped."

"You don't have to tell me if you don't want."

"Maybe it'll help get it off my chest." She picked at the hem of her blouse and continued her story. "When he leaned over and kissed my cheek, I thought—how sweet. But then he whispered an apology and bolted. Left me standing there alone with my entire hometown in attendance."

What a jerk. Kyle must have known he wasn't going to marry her before then. Why not call it off before the ceremony? Instead, he'd made her humiliation a public ordeal.

"And everyone feels sorry for you?" He willed himself not to put his arm around her. To offer comfort and protection. "Did y'all have a fight before the ceremony?"

"No." She shrugged. "We never even had a disagreement. Whenever I didn't see eye to eye with him, he always sidetracked me."

"You have no idea why he bailed?" He grimaced. "I mean, why he—"

"*Bailed* works." Her small hand fisted. "He humiliated me on center stage, then waltzed off and found someone else. Like nothing ever happened. Like I never mattered."

"You matter. And he's a jerk."

"I've forgiven him, but forgetting is harder." She looked up at him, her eyes glossy.

But he needed to tread carefully with her. So she wasn't a scammer, a player or a gold digger. But she was obviously still hung up on her ex. Never mind what a busted romance with his business partner would do to the dude ranch.

"I can't stand to even think about going back home." She hung her head. "Especially in light of his engagement, to attend a wedding with everybody watching to see how I handle it."

"No one would blame you if you didn't go." He tried to fill his tone with empathy, not pity.

"True." She traced her fingers over the chain of the swing. "But if I don't go, the whole state of Texas will figure getting dumped at the altar scarred me so badly I couldn't attend my own cousin's wedding."

"The whole state, huh?"

"All of the twenty-five hundred or so in Aubrey, anyway." She blew out a shuddery breath. "He ruined everything. I can't even go home and hold my head up." She leaned against him ever so slightly, her shoulder against his.

He'd kept his distance as long as he could and rested his cheek against her temple. With her tangle of waves soft against his jaw, his pulse ratcheted up a notch.

A Christian, outdoorsy, didn't-mind-getting-dirty, low-maintenance-yet-beautiful woman sat right next to him. One that loved and missed his sister as much as he did. How much more perfect could Landry be?

But she was hurting over another man, and rebound relationships never worked out. Yet here he was—getting too close.

His family legacy was in jeopardy, as he'd learn the extent of the tree damage tomorrow. Yet the most pressing thing on his mind—was Landry. He'd fought his feelings for her tooth and nail. To no avail.

She straightened. "I better go freshen up for Bible study."

"It's not my turn or I'd go with you." Did she hear the regret in his voice?

"See ya." She waved her fingers at him and stepped inside.

Maybe he should give up. Stop fighting it. Win her heart. Make her forget all about the man who'd broken it.

A dozen foresters teemed at the dude ranch property line as Landry's nerves buzzed. Chase had tried to ditch her on his way out of the ranch house that morning, but she'd managed to catch up with him just as he was leaving. Had he intentionally tried to give her the slip? Or was he just flustered?

Try as she might to be calm, cool and collected, she could feel how keyed up Chase was, too. The dark circles under his bloodshot eyes told of his sleepless night.

"It's gonna be okay." She rested her hand on his arm. "I've been praying about it."

"Me, too."

The only serene property owner was Resa. "It really will be okay." She gave them a thousand-watt smile.

Men and women dressed in tan shirts and olive pants inspected the stricken trees along with their surroundings on both sides of the fence.

Landry tried to see what they saw. The three live oaks on their side had patches of brown, but she saw a few brown leaves on at least five trees on Resa's side. Was that oak wilt or just lack of rain?

One of the male foresters headed their way, and she heard Chase suck in a deep breath.

"We've concluded our inspection. You have a total of five diseased trees, and Ms. McCall has seven." The inspector handed them each an invoice.

Bigger numbers than what she'd hoped for, but not as bad as Chase had imagined.

The inspector went on to explain how much the forest service would cover. Since Resa was responsible for her share, what was left was manageable.

"Thank you." Chase shook the inspector's hand as the workers gathered their testing supplies.

"That's not too bad." Landry linked arms with him, relief unwinding the knot in her gut. "We won't have to worry about a loan."

"I can cover y'all." Resa grabbed the invoice from him.

Landry let go of him and snatched it back. "You most certainly will not."

"But you heard them—this originated from a tree on my property. And I'm just thankful Chase caught it early."

"You're not paying for our part." Chase nabbed the invoice from Landry. "It's not your fault some insect carried a diseased spore to one of your trees instead of ours."

"What if I front y'all the funds?" Resa scanned the trees. "Y'all could pay me back."

"We're okay, Resa." Chase's tone was firm. "We can handle this. It's not as bad I expected."

"All right." Resa shaded her eyes. "But if y'all get in a bind, please let me know."

"We're good." Chase folded the invoice, shoved it in his pocket. "Landry implemented a special rate for the summer, and we've had a guest boom. And there's no telling what she's got up her sleeve for the off-season."

"No pressure." Landry let out a wry chuckle.

Resa pointed at her. "You still haven't called me for lunch."

"I will. We've just been busy."

"Let her loose for an hour, slave driver." Resa hugged Chase, then Landry, and strolled to her car.

Chase ran his hands through his hair. "This won't hurt the business account."

"I have a nice nest egg."

"There's no need for that."

"The business account has been built up by your family. I haven't contributed until recently. I insist on covering half the cost."

"You've got it—without putting you between a rock and a hard place?"

"I have it."

"All right. If you insist." He steered her toward his truck. "I'm so relieved it wasn't worse."

"I knew it would work out. You need to be more positive, Johnny Rain Cloud."

"Hey, I'm the one with the 'Happy Trails' ringtone." He blew out a big breath. "It's just that Eden was so much better at this." He kicked at a dust clod. "Making big decisions stresses me out. Running the dude ranch was never my dream. It was hers."

She'd known it. Had tried to ignore it since she'd gotten to the point of liking him. "Do you regret coming home when you did?" Her voice barely a whisper. Afraid to hear his answer.

"I can't cut out on my family legacy. Either run it or sell it, and I don't want either choice."

"Or have someone else run it for you. You could be my silent partner." Since she'd arrived, she'd gone from trying to win him over to liking, respecting and relying on him. If he left, she'd miss him.

"I'll be fine." He opened the truck door for her. "Don't worry about it. Maybe things will settle down now."

She climbed up, watched him go around to get in.
How long could he stay and be so unhappy? And
if he left, what would she do without him?

Chapter Nine

It was Chase's favorite part of the day. A fine Friday morning, before anyone else stirred. Especially now, since his nerves had been in a jumble lately. But with the tree problem settled now, he'd slept soundly last night. He grabbed his coffee, locked his cabin door and strolled to the ranch house.

And Landry was already there. In his spot, slowly swaying on the porch swing. It wasn't the first time. It used to frustrate him when she invaded his space. Now he was glad to get to spend time with her.

"Mind if I join you?"

She scooted over to make room for him. "Morning."

Birdsong ushered in the day. The quiet chatter of ranch hands mixed with whinnies and the clop of hooves came from the barn.

"I'm leaving for my cousin's wedding tomorrow." She sipped her coffee, looked up at him. "Under extreme duress."

"Mom mentioned we'd be shorthanded." He'd miss her. And not just her work ethic. But maybe he didn't have to… He could escort her, support her through it. A great way to make himself indispensable to her. Better yet, he could save her day.

"About that." He waggled his eyebrows at her. "I might have a brilliant idea."

"Pretend I have the flu."

He chuckled. "Better. I could take you." He ducked his head, afraid to watch her reaction. "Act like we're a couple."

"What?" She snorted.

"You said half your hometown probably thinks we're a couple by now."

"True."

"We'll go to the wedding and let everyone think what they want." He set the swing in motion again. "If I'm your plus one, you won't have to field questions about your love life. You can show them you've moved on—that you don't need their pity."

"I have moved on. I left Aubrey, and I've proven I don't need a husband to be happy." She stood, propped her hands on her hips. "But apparently you think I'm so pathetic, I need a pretend boyfriend."

"That's not what I meant. Will you sit down and listen?" She might not think of her hair as fiery, but her temper sure was.

"You feel sorry for me, just like everybody else." She spun away, headed for the door.

"I don't. If I feel sorry for anyone, it's what's-his-name. He's the pathetic one for letting you get away."

That stopped her. "Really?"

"Scout's honor."

"Thanks." She blew out a shuddery breath, faced him again. "Sorry. Sore subject."

He patted the seat beside him.

"I really am over him. It was just so humiliating." She reclaimed her spot. "Weddings are supposed to be such a joyous occasion. But after Kyle—and Eden...since then, the thought of weddings makes me sad."

"I'm right there with you." The muscle in Chase's jaw tensed up. "For the longest time, I avoided the backyard. I had to work at reminding myself of how happy Eden was on her wedding day." How happy she must have been on her honeymoon.

"Sometimes when I look at this tree-shaded expanse of green, I can still hear her laughter." She closed her eyes.

"Me, too." He twined his fingers with hers. "Listen, weddings are tough for you. And this one will be especially brutal. Let me support you through it."

"We're talking a six-hour drive."

"Isn't stuff like this what friends are for?"

"That's really sweet." She squeezed his hand. "Tell you what? We'll check with your folks. If both of us going won't leave them in a bind, I'll take you up on the offer."

He stood, strolled to the back door and stuck his head in the kitchen where neither of his parents looked up from their work. "Can y'all do without me if I go to Aubrey with Landry?"

"Danny's been wanting more hours since the new baby." Mom glanced up long enough to reveal a satisfied grin.

He should've spared the details. Just asked for the day off, not mentioned they'd be doing a road trip together.

He aimed a glower at her, shut the door and reclaimed his seat by Landry. "We're good to go."

"But I haven't agreed to the pretend thing." A doe with her fawn crossed the trail at the edge of the woods. "I can't believe you wanted to turn hunters loose on them," she whispered.

"I'll admit, they are beautiful." The doe stilled, caught sight of them, nudged her fawn, and they bolted into the woods. "If we're gonna do this, we need to make sure we know pertinent details about each other. Things couples would know."

"I'm not saying I'm in on this make-believe relationship." She wouldn't look at him. "But what kind of things?"

"Your favorite color is that blue-green jewelry stone color, right?"

"Turquoise." Her gaze met his. "How do you know?"

He shrugged. "You wear it often."

"I'm guessing yours is red. Because of your truck."

"Very good. For the record, my favorite car is a Mustang—preferably red. But it's highly impractical to own a car on a ranch. So I have a red Dodge Ram with a lift kit instead. Arr arr." He made a macho grunting sound.

She rolled her eyes. "Now that your little he-man moment is over, what else?"

"Your favorite hymn is 'The Old Rugged Cross.'"

"You've heard me hum it. And I've heard you whistle 'Blessed Assurance.'"

"It's my favorite. Let's talk flowers." He tapped his chin with his finger. "Those purple things that hang from stuff in the spring. What's it called?"

"Wisteria, and they're lavender. But how did you—?"

"I might have sort of Googled you." He grimaced.

She whacked his shoulder. "You did what?"

"When you first arrived." He splayed his hands. "I thought you were a scammer."

"Oh, no." She leaned her head back, closed her eyes. "You saw my mindless blatherings about the wedding that never happened."

"You mean the happy plans of a woman in love." Though his stomach turned at the notion, he gave her arm a reassuring squeeze.

"I thought I was." Her voice cracked. "I closed my account after we ran into him. I wish I'd done it sooner. This is too embarrassing."

"We're not finished here." He pressed his fingers to his temple as if he could lock in the information. "I have to remember. Turquoise, lavender wisteria."

"I don't think it's unusual for a guy to struggle with color and flower names." She giggled.

He'd never noticed how cute her laugh was. "Your greatest fear is a bug getting in your ear."

The smile slid from her face. "How did you know that?"

"Eden told me about y'all's trail ride. About you dashing inside, squealing and jumping while pounding your head with your palm. Granny dragging you to the sink to run water in your ear."

"The moth floated right out." She shivered, clamped a hand over her ear. "I can still feel it in there."

"I noticed you never uncover your ears, even when you wear a ponytail." Why did he suddenly have to urge run his fingers through her silky curls?

"Your biggest fear already happened." She snagged his gaze. "Losing someone you love."

He couldn't swallow the lump in his throat.

Something warm settled in her eyes. "We probably know more about each other than most people."

Sitting here with her was feeling way too right. "Now all we need is a story," he said.

"What kind of story?"

"We'll cause a stir at the wedding." She muddled his thinking. Would he even have to do any pretending for the wedding? "We need to know when our relationship became more than friendship. That kind of thing."

"More lies," Her gaze swung to his.

"Not necessarily. We can be honest about how we've gotten closer since inheriting the dude ranch."

She chuckled. "At least you don't think I'm a con artist anymore."

"It took two weeks to fall for each other."

"That's awfully fast."

"Sometimes it happens that fast. But you've pretty much been here a few days past two weeks, so we'll have to go with it." He had to look away. Because coming up with this story, the reasons he had for not falling for Landry were starting to give way. "We should have a favorite movie. Ever seen that *Star Trek* movie where Khan put that worm thing in Chekov's ear?"

"Stop it." She whacked his shoulder.

"Just trying to help you overcome your fear."

"Yeah, right." She smacked him again. "But I could go for watching *The Twilight Zone*."

"What's your favorite episode?"

"The one with Burgess Meredith where all he wants to do is…"

"Have time to read. Classic. Such irony."

She turned serious on him. "I'll think about the pretending thing. Let you know tomorrow. But either way, I appreciate you going with me. It means a lot."

"Fair enough." Watching her every move, every expression. He was coming to realize that no woman had ever affected him the way she did.

"Can we leave at six in the morning? I know it's early, but the ceremony is at two, and I'd like to have extra time in case anything goes wrong."

"I'll be ready."

If he could convince her to do this, he'd have to remind his heart not to forget they were pretending.

The next day, they were halfway to Aubrey and Landry's insides continued to whir. Should she take Chase up on his offer—pretend they were a couple? He hadn't brought it up again. Just made small talk as he drove.

The opportunity to stop hiding her growing feelings for him tugged at her. At least for a day. If she agreed to the pretense—how would her family react? Should she pull them aside, let them in on the ruse? Would they go along with it if they knew? It was lying.

But her feelings were becoming real. And that

was the biggest problem of all. If she spent a day playing couple with Chase, would she be able to get back to normal with him afterward? She wasn't sure her heart could handle the charade.

Her cell phone buzzed, making her jump. She quickly dug it out of her pocket.

"Just for the record," Chase said, never taking his eyes off the road, "that's a really boring ringtone."

"It's my sister." She swiped her finger across the screen. "Hey, Devree. What's up?"

"Waverly called the wedding off. She dumped Kyle."

Laughter bubbled out of Landry. "You're kidding. You're certain about this?"

"Another wedding planner called to let me know the venue they booked is up for grabs next month." Devree sighed. "Please tell me you won't go running back to him if he beckons."

"Trust me. You have nothing to worry about."

"Good." Relief tinged her tone. "Are you on your way?"

"Yeah. About halfway there."

"Can't wait to see you."

"Me, too." She ended the call, slid her phone back into her pocket. "Kyle is single."

"What?" Chase glanced her direction.

"His fiancée cancelled the wedding." She snorted. "That's the best news I've heard in I don't even know how long." She knew exactly how Kyle must feel. She should have been empathetic toward him, especially since she'd forgiven him. But all she felt was validation.

"Congratulations." Chase's mouth tightened.

"This will make the wedding better for me." No need for the pretense. Her hometown would be buzzing with the breakup. Taking the pressure off her. She closed her eyes. "I've made a decision."

"About what?" His jaw clenched.

"There won't be any pretending. I'll make sure everyone in Aubrey knows we're just friends."

"It would still make the wedding easier for you if we pretend. Just one wedding, and then we could pretend to break up later. By then, your hometown would be convinced you'd moved on."

"I'm not comfortable with it." She shook her head. "I should never have considered it to begin with."

"Fine. Let me know if you change your mind."

"I won't." But something inside her died at her assertion. She'd just blown the chance to spend a day getting cozy with Chase. Something she'd looked forward to—even if it wouldn't have been real. For him, anyway.

It was the perfect Saturday for a wedding. Bright sunshine warmed this first day of August. Chase stood on the lawn of Landry's home church. Their six-hour drive had been mostly quiet after Devree's call. Lost in their own thoughts and interrupted only by necessities like stopping for gas and food. As if a wall had been erected between them.

Kyle got what he deserved. And Chase had to hand it to the blonde for putting him in his place. Justice well served. He could roar with laughter over it.

Except that Landry was way too happy over the news. He couldn't do this. Couldn't watch her celebrate Kyle's freedom. Instead of having the chance to see what a relationship between them could be like, Landry would introduce Chase as her friend. Did she decide that so Kyle wouldn't get word about her bringing a plus one?

Was she already hoping he'd come back to her now? Would he ask her to? Would she take him back if he did?

Chase's gut wrenched. If Kyle came slithering back and Landry fell for him again, Chase would be stuck watching the romance unfold. Why did Landry still have feelings for that jerk? How had Kyle gotten not one, but two women to fall for him?

In just two and a half weeks, Landry had turned Chase upside down.

Just get through the wedding. Why did he feel like he was losing her, when he'd never even had her?

A hand clapped him on the back. "Howdy, Chase." Clay Warren adjusted his cowboy hat. His wife, Rayna, by his side.

"How are y'all?" Surreal. But Landry had Chase too tied up in knots to be speechless over his hero.

"Good. Where's Landry?" Rayna looked around.

"She's here somewhere." He scanned the crowd but didn't spot her. "Probably helping the bride get ready."

"Must be hard on her after Kyle." Rayna shaded her eyes with her hand. "Especially with his engagement and then breakup."

"Yeah." Even more so since she still loved him.

"At least Ally's wedding is here at this church and not at the scene of the crime, the Ever After Chapel." Rayna huffed out a sigh. "How do you think she's holding up?"

"She's tough. I'll get her through it."

Rayna patted his shoulder. "You sure there's nothing between y'all?"

"We're just friends."

"I know several very happy couples who started out as friends." She gave him a conspiratorial wink.

"We'd better find seats," Clay said. "Looks like the place is filling up. The groom's my cousin, so we're sitting on his side." Clay offered his arm, and Rayna settled her hand in the crook of his elbow. He looked at Chase. "You coming?"

"Sure. I think Landry's dad saved me a seat." He followed the couple up the steps.

Her dad was seated about halfway up on the left—apparently that was the bride's side.

He approached her dad. Tina's purse and Owen's jacket were scattered down the length of the pew.

"We saved a seat for you and Landry." Owen moved his wife's purse for him, and he settled in. Leaving a space on each side of her dad for his wife and daughter.

The smell of mothballs invaded his space. Owen twisted in his seat to look behind him. An elderly woman leaned over the back of their pew.

"Mrs. Thornbury. How nice to see you." Owen gestured to Chase. "This is everyone's favorite Sunday school teacher. She's led half the kids in Aubrey to the Lord."

"I give God all the credit." Mrs. Thornbury peered at Chase.

"Nice to meet you. Chase Donovan. Landry's business partner." Though he wished he could say different.

"Is our dear Landry here?" Her hand settled on his shoulder. Kind eyes.

"Yes."

"Oh, my. This must be hard on her. Poor thing." Her concern was genuine. "You sure it's just a business thing? Do I hear more wedding bells on the horizon?"

I wish. He patted her arthritic fingers. "Landry and I are only friends."

"Oh. Well, you tell her I said that uppity fellow

wasn't worthy of her. She can do better." Her hand dropped away from him.

"I will." But he wouldn't. Landry didn't need to know everyone still felt sorry for her. How could he protect her now that Kyle was free. His fists clenched.

If only he could have talked her into going ahead with their pretend relationship for the wedding. Simply because he longed to let his real feelings show.

Mama, Devree and Aunt Dianne surrounded Ally with makeup brushes, combs and hair spray. Landry stayed out of the way with Ally's best friend.

"That's enough." Her cousin held her hands up like a shield. "My hair and makeup have never been this precise."

The ladies quickly backed off.

Dianne picked up the hair spray again. "It's your wedding day. I just want my baby girl to look stunning."

"But I want Cody to recognize me when I walk down the aisle." Ally grabbed the hair spray out of her mom's hand.

Landry snickered. Ally stood, gathered her billowing skirt and turned to face her.

"I'm so glad you came." Ally hugged her. "I know it's rough."

"I wouldn't miss it."

"I would have asked you to be a bridesmaid, but…"

"I know. It's fine. I'm happy to be here and so happy for you."

Ally pulled away, swiped her cheeks.

"No crying." Caitlyn, Ally's best friend, moved in on the bride and dabbed a tissue under her eyes.

"I can't think of anyone more deserving of getting dumped than Kyle." Ally guffawed.

"I know. Except that—from what I saw—they were perfect for each other." Landry clamped her mouth shut. "I have to stop that. I forgave him, so I shouldn't be happy he's hurting."

"I'm still praying about forgiving him." Mama huffed. "Thankfully God is patient with a mama when some jerk hurts her baby girl."

Landry's smile died. Maybe that's why Chase had clammed up during their drive. Maybe he didn't approve of her laughing over Kyle's broken engagement.

"I don't want to talk about Kyle." She closed her eyes. "Or think about him. This is Ally's day. We should focus on her."

"I've had enough focus." Ally rolled her eyes. "Besides, Landry has moved on. Found someone better than what's-his-name in Chase."

"No." Landry held her hands up. "We're only business partners. And friends."

"Oh." Ally frowned. "Well, after Rayna and

Clay saw y'all in Medina, the whole town was buzzing."

"We were just running errands for the dude ranch and squeezed lunch in. That's all Rayna saw. I've known him only a short time, and we're developing a nice friendship. That's all."

"Trust me—" Ally's dreamy smile lit her entire face "—a friendship can turn into the most amazing love you've ever imagined."

If both people were interested in becoming a couple. But Chase wasn't. And Landry was still too afraid to trust what she felt.

"He's way too good-looking to be *just* friends with." Devree's intense gaze dissected her.

Landry tried not to fidget. "I'd better go find a seat." She gave Ally another hug. "I love you and you look gorgeous, but no more than usual. Cody is a blessed man."

She blew a kiss to the entire lot of her female family members, then exited the classroom and wove her way through the lobby. At the doors to the sanctuary, she stopped. Chase sat near her dad, the seat between them unoccupied, waiting for her. Landry took a deep breath, straightened her shoulders and tried for casual as she strode to the pew.

"Excuse me," she whispered to her dad. He stood and kissed her check as she shuffled past him and settled beside Chase.

He was wearing a typical cowboy suit made up of a Western blazer, jeans and boots. Look-

ing way too handsome. And sitting way too close.
She closed her eyes. But it didn't do any good.
His woodsy cologne filled her senses. He smelled
as good as he looked. Solid, dependable and fun-
loving all wrapped up in one handsome cowboy
package.

Feelings she'd never had for anyone before
swirled around. She'd finally met a really great
guy. But she wasn't sure she could trust her befuddled heart.

"I heard they're dating," someone behind them
whispered.

Her eyes popped open, and she looked up at
Chase.

"Really?" another lady's voice reached her. "I'm
so glad she moved on. They make a cute couple."

"I heard that despicable ex-fiancé of hers is already engaged again."

"No. They broke up."

"Well, I don't guess it will matter to Landry
now."

Neither voice sounded familiar. Just as she was
about to turn around and set them straight, she
heard music start up and the bridesmaids began
to trail down the aisle. Then the wedding march
began, and the crowd stood. Chase touched her
elbow and urged her to her feet.

She'd get a glimpse of them after the wedding
and make sure they knew the truth about her relationship with Chase at the reception. In the mean-

time, she had to focus on Ally's ceremony. And keep her feelings buried.

If Chase figured her out, would he still be comfortable owning a business with her? Or, just when they were learning how to compromise on the dude ranch, would he tell her to find herself another partner? In more ways than one?

Chapter Ten

Tables and chairs lined the churchyard, with filmy fabric and red roses draped everywhere. What were they thinking, having an outdoor reception this time of year? The sun shone hot from the clear Texas sky, leaving the guests fanning. At least Chase was used to it, but his jacket was wanting to come off as he sat at their table waiting for the wedding party to join the reception.

The bride and groom exited the church, followed by their attendants and Landry. The family picture session obviously over. He saw her scan the gathering, spot him, head his way. Her ruffled pale turquoise skirt skimmed her knees in the front, then dipped low down the sides and brushed the heels of her cowgirl boots in the back. Way too pretty for comfort.

Of course, he thought she was beautiful even when she wore her disposable food prep cap at the dude ranch. But today, her hair hung long and loose, wild curls in disarray.

She smiled down at him, turning his insides to pudding. "Is this seat taken?"

Words wouldn't come. He shook his head.

She claimed the chair beside him as her flowery perfume caught up with him.

"Landry, introduce me to your young man." A silver-haired woman about midsixties set her hand on Chase's arm.

"He's not my young man, Dotty. You remember me talking about my friend Eden from Bandera. This is her brother, Chase."

"I wish I had a friend with a brother who looked like him when I was your age." Her puckered lips formed a small O. "He's the one you inherited the dude ranch with?"

"Yes. We're business partners. That's all." She turned to Chase. "Dotty works at Clay's ranch."

"It's a shame to be *just* business partners with such a fine-looking cowboy. I'd rethink that if I were you, young lady." Dotty shot him a wink.

Chase's neck heated as Dotty ambled past them.

"Are you blushing?" Landry chuckled.

"No." He cleared his throat. "Of course not."

"I almost said you were my friend. But that can be code for boyfriend." She scanned the crowd. "I guess it doesn't matter what I tell them. They all assume we're dating. I appreciate you coming, but maybe this wasn't such a good idea." Her gaze crashed into his.

If she'd gotten her sister's call about Kyle before they'd left this morning, he probably wouldn't have been here.

He shoved his hands in his pockets, striving for casual. "People think what they want. Eventually they'll catch on, or someone who knows us will set them straight. Don't worry about it."

"I wanted to tell those ladies who were talking about us the truth. But I never saw them after the ceremony. Did you?"

"No. They must have left."

"I'm so happy for y'all." A young woman clapped her hands, then bent to hug Landry. "Y'all are just the most perfect couple I've ever seen."

"But," Landry sputtered, "we're not—"

"This right here is just what you needed to mend a broken heart." The woman gave his shoulders a squeeze. "I just wish you could have found him before you ran into Mister Stuffed Shirt."

"Chase and I are business partners. That's all."

"Sure you are." The woman giggled. "It looks like the bride and groom are getting ready to leave. Come on, Landry. Maybe you'll catch the bouquet and officially land Mr. Fine Cowboy here."

The woman linked arms with her and hauled her up, then hurried across the lawn.

He knew that whether Landry caught the bouquet or not, he had a lot of work to do for a chance at eventually becoming her groom.

He closed his eyes and, just for a moment, allowed himself to imagine her catching those flowers, then flashing him a knee-jolting smile.

A hand patted his shoulder, jarred him from the fantasy. He opened his eyes.

Tina's gaze locked with his. A tiny smile lifted the corners of her mouth. "It's good to see you again. Good to see y'all together. To see our Landry happy."

Was Landry's mom letting him know he should pursue her daughter? Even if she was, Tina's approval didn't mean Landry would be receptive. Maybe he should bide his time. Give her time to heal. But with Kyle a free man, could he afford to?

If only she could bail. But here she was, standing with the other single women, ready to scoop up the bouquet. Only Landry didn't want it.

Yet this was her chance to prove to her hometown that she wasn't still pining for Kyle. That she wasn't too embarrassed to attend her cousin's wedding. She wasn't too scarred to participate in this long-held tradition. Or too terrified to give love a second chance. Even though she was.

Ally turned her back and flung the bouquet, and Landry dove for it. In front of three women she used to work with. The blossoms grazed her fingers, and she latched on with both hands.

"I got it." She did her version of a quarterback victory dance after a winning touchdown. The gathering applauded. She'd shown them—she was so over it.

"Way to go, Landry," her cousin's husband boomed over the microphone, pumping his fist. "And watch out, Chase. I think your gal's got a wedding on her mind."

Her face went hot and Ally's eyes widened, obviously feeling Landry's discomfort, as the gathering continued to applaud, turning in Chase's direction.

"No. We're not dating. Only friends." But her protests didn't get anywhere without the sound system. Maybe if she announced it over the microphone.

Chase strolled toward her. Maybe everyone would be able to hear him.

But he pulled her close. Before she could blink, his lips were on hers. A sweet, tender kiss and her brain fogged. All resistance melted and she kissed him back.

He pulled away, a message in his gaze she couldn't quite read. "Um, we have an audience."

Oh, that. Skin steaming with embarrassment—she looked around. Stunned silence seemed to have attacked the other guests. Until applause broke out.

Landry's gaze dropped to his chest. Why had he kissed her? Why had she kissed him back?

"Oh, my." A familiar voice. Mama. "Looks like we missed something."

Landry's eyes widened, met Chase's again. It took everything she had to pull away from him.

She took a step back, blinked, tugged her gaze from his.

She looked over to her father and saw his face vibrant red. He'd drilled it into his daughters' heads, no public displays of affection. She gave a weak smile. Did her legs even still work? She slid her hand into the crook of Chase's elbow just so she wouldn't tip over. Tried to blend in since she'd practically taken over Ally's reception.

The buzz of conversation started up again. Probably most of it about that kiss.

Devree—coming in fast. "I knew it."

"Not now," Landry whispered.

"Then when?"

"I'll call you. Tomorrow." Maybe by then, she could think straight again.

"You better. If you don't, I'll call you, and I'll make you spill even if Chase is sitting right there listening."

Cody cleared his throat over the PA. "My lovely bride and I appreciate y'all sharing the happiest day of our lives. But if it's all the same to y'all, I'm ready to blow this joint." He grabbed Ally's hand, and together they dashed off the podium as the crowd surged toward them, pelting their backs with birdseed.

A few older couples who hadn't gone chasing after the newlyweds ambled past.

"Come on, Landry." Chase led her toward the parking lot.

Just resting her hand on his arm lit a spark. How could he affect her so? He was Chase. Her business partner.

His kiss lit her up like a Texas Lone Star.

If only she could trust her heart. To know if she really loved him. Or not.

Chase let loose a joyous guffaw as he started the engine. His breath stalled. What had he just done? How could he cover?

"Why exactly did you do that?"

Play it cool. "Sometimes a laugh just won't do."

"Not that. Why did you kiss me?"

Because he couldn't hold back a second longer. "Did you see their faces?"

"How could I not?" She groaned. "We were the center of attention. What got into you?"

You. You got into me. "I was standing there listening to a group of women giggle about your wedding fail." Discussing whether Landry would go chasing after Kyle since he was single again. "I'd had enough and I figured you had, too." But the main reason he'd kissed her was that he'd really wanted to.

He couldn't just roll over, play dead and wait for Kyle to come win her back. He'd seen an opening and taken it. Hoped his kiss might sway her in his direction.

"What women?"

"How am I supposed to know? About your age. Jealous and catty."

"Probably Cyndi Hempstead. Sounds like her crew."

"Resident mean girl?"

"Every town has one."

"Well, we gave ole Cyndi plenty to contemplate on." He shot her a wink. "I could tell exactly when you decided to go along with me." For one ecstatic moment, he'd thought his tactics had worked. But apparently not. His stomach clenched as he made light of it. If only it had been real.

Her face went crimson. "You should have seen my father's face. He doesn't approve of public displays."

Disappointment settled heavy in his gut. Her embarrassed look revealed her true feelings. She was ashamed, and apparently it hadn't meant anything to her. While she turned him inside out, she felt nothing.

"You broke the rules." She slipped one boot off. And stirred up a cloud of floral perfume in the process. "I told you I didn't want to pretend at the wedding."

"Some rules are meant to be broken." Chase merged onto the interstate. "Put your seat belt on."

"Just give me a minute," she snapped. Then she slipped off the other boot and chucked them in the backseat. She adjusted her skirt to sit on one foot.

"I'm sorry." He sighed, gave up trying to make her laugh. "I was just trying to help."

"Why does you helping involve a kiss in front of the entire town?" She buckled up, adjusted the strap on her shoulder. "Maybe if we each tackle half the Aubrey phone book, we could call each household and tell them we're just friends."

"It's not a big deal."

"I can't believe Cody said that. He's always been a big jokester, but he took it too far."

"He probably really thought we're dating." He could barely concentrate with her beside him. "And nobody would listen when you tried to correct them anyway. It'll die down eventually."

If only the ache in his chest would do the same. But her determination to get the truth out about their relationship was like a dagger to his heart.

The least he could do was explain himself to her dad. "I guess there is one call I need to make. Can you dial your dad's number for me?"

Her laugh was sarcastic. "Not unless you tell me what you plan to say to him."

"I need to clear up the kiss thing. Apologize to him."

She looked out the passenger window a few seconds, then dug out her phone, swiped the screen, held it toward him. "It's on speaker."

"Thanks." It rang three times.

"Landry? Is everything okay?" Her dad's worried voice.

"Everything's fine, Mr. Malone. This is Chase Donovan. I'm just using her phone to set something straight, to apologize." He gripped the steering wheel—white-knuckled with both hands. "I'm really sorry about my actions today. I shouldn't have kissed your daughter in public."

"I hope it won't happen again."

"It won't, sir." But he wished it could. "You see, Landry and I are only friends."

"It didn't look that way from where I stood."

"I'd just heard people talk all day about how Kyle dumped her." He chanced a glance at her, but she stared out the passenger window. "I thought they needed new subject fodder. But I didn't think about how it might embarrass you. Or Landry. She blasted me as soon as we got in the truck."

"I'm sure she did. But your heart was in the right place." Her dad's tone softened.

"I knew you'd understand the situation, Mr. Malone. I apologize for any embarrassment."

"I appreciate that. You definitely gave them something to talk about." Owen chuckled. "You and Landry were pretty convincing. Maybe this will stop the Kyle chatter around here. He's a jerk." Her dad's tone echoed his dislike.

"I'd better let you get back to your day. It was nice talking to you."

"You, too."

The line went dead. That had been the biggest

pack of lies Chase had ever told. He would never regret kissing her.

"Thank you for that." She turned to face him. "I guess all of Aubrey is convinced I'm over Kyle at least."

If only she really was. "Even without me in the equation, that little chicken dance of yours cinched it."

She covered her face. "I can't believe I did that."

"Me, neither. You got some moves I knew nothing about."

"I was just so pumped. At first I was like—if I never see another bridal bouquet again, it'll be too soon. But then it hit me. If I killed myself trying to catch it, everyone would figure I was over Kyle." She closed her eyes. "I just never thought about you getting dragged into it."

And he'd never realized how much it would hurt for him to get dragged into it. For a moment he'd held Landry in his arms. But it would never happen again.

"Can we go fishing this week?" she asked. "Any day when you don't have guide trips scheduled. The river isn't far from the ranch house. If someone needs us, we could be there quickly. Some day when it's slow, maybe Becca could cover the office."

Huh? "We just caught a boatload and got them processed. Our freezer's full."

"We could catch and release. Eden and I used to do that. Just for fun."

Sitting side by side on the dock with her would be torture. With her feeling nothing and him feeling everything.

"I just thought it would be fun." She shrugged. "After all the stress we've had lately, a nice, relaxing day of fishing."

"Sure." But anything involving her wouldn't be relaxing for him. How could he act normal with her again when everything inside him had changed?

If he was patient, extremely patient, and Landry's feelings for Kyle eventually subsided, could Chase have a chance with her? Maybe someday in the distant future. For now, he'd just have to hold on to that hope. And pray Kyle stayed out of her picture in the meantime.

Landry pulled into the furniture store parking lot and noticed movement at the front door as Resa unlocked it to let her in.

She drew in a big breath, got out of the car. It was the second day of August, and waves of heat rose from the asphalt.

The bell dinged as Resa held the door open for her.

"There you are." Resa gave her a hug and clicked the lock in place. "I'm so glad we're finally getting to do lunch." Her thousand-watt smile proved she meant it.

The massive log footboard in the center of the store drew Landry. She ran her hand over the smooth wood. It always amazed her how something that still looked like a tree could be transformed into splinter-free furniture.

"Please tell me the dude ranch is hopping, you're building cabins and you want to place a gargantuan order over lunch." She was all porcelain skin and contrasting raven hair, yet Resa had no idea how beautiful she was. Inside and out.

"I wish." Landry scanned the store filled with one-of-a-kind log furniture and rustic designer bedding. "Business has picked up, but we're not there yet. I'd love to add cabins. Eventually."

"You okay?" Resa linked arms with her.

"Got a minute before we head out?"

"Sure." Resa led her to the back of the store and they settled across from each other at her massive cedar desk. "I'm guessing from the worry lines on your face Chase is giving you a hard time."

Resa had proved herself a caring and confidential sounding board in the past. And she couldn't talk about this with Devree. If her family got wind of her feelings for Chase, they'd torment her with questions she didn't have answers for.

Landry started at the beginning with Kyle dumping her, then learning about his engagement, seeing him in San Antonio and Chase pretending they were a couple. "After that, Chase and I were building a tentative friendship."

"Until?" Resa raised an eyebrow.

"Chase went to my cousin's wedding with me yesterday." She filled in the details, then blew out a big sigh, squeezed her eyes closed. "He kissed me."

Resa's jaw dropped. "He did what?"

"It was a pretend kiss." But it sure felt real.

"What did you do?"

"I was confused at first."

"And then what?" Resa leaned toward her.

"I kissed him back." Her face warmed.

Resa's eyes widened. "Because you realized he was trying to show everyone you'd moved on?"

"No. I didn't know anyone else existed until Chase ended the kiss." She covered her face with her hands.

"Maybe there's more than friendship between y'all."

"There can't be. He's my business partner." Landry's gaze dropped to the desk, then pinged back to meet Resa's. "We can't be anything more than friends. How could a pretend kiss melt my brain?"

"Well, he is one fine cowboy." Resa stifled a chuckle. "So did y'all talk about it?"

"He thinks I was pretending, too, despite the fact that I snuggled up to him like dust on a mini-blind."

Resa dissolved into giggles.

"It's not funny." Landry shot her the evil eye. "Do not laugh."

"Sorry." Resa's mouth twitched. She swallowed hard, leaned back in her chair again, scrutinized Landry. "Did it freak him out like it did you?"

"I don't know, I was too busy being blown away." She buried her face in her hands again. "In six weeks, we have to decide what to do with the dude ranch."

She stood, paced in front of Resa's desk. "If we entertain the idea of a relationship and it doesn't work out, how uncomfortable would that be? The awkward meter is already off the charts as it is."

"And besides—" her steps faltered "—I don't trust myself. Obviously I wouldn't know love if it kicked me in the teeth."

"You can't let one loser keep you from taking a chance on love again."

"Look who's talking, Miss I Don't Date. If you think Chase is so fine, why don't you go for him?" Something sank in her stomach. Why had she said that? She didn't want anybody going for Chase. Especially not her friend.

"Because I'm not interested in dating. Him or anyone." Resa's gaze dropped to the desk. "But we're not talking about me. You and Chase have a close bond—through Eden. I think y'all could be a great couple."

"Well, I don't."

"There's a thin line between friendship and love." Resa's tone softened, her unseeing gaze shifting to something obviously in the past.

"That sounded like experience talking." Landry reclaimed her seat. "Have you ever had a *friend*?"

"Once." Resa focused on her again. "A long time ago. I thought—" She shook her head. "But he turned out not to be the man I thought he was."

"Want to talk about it?"

"Maybe someday." A sad smile settled on Resa's lips. "But in the meantime—I don't think you should rule out more than friendship with Chase. He's just what he seems. Solid, dependable and sweet."

"It can't happen. For a whole host of reasons." Landry leaned back in her chair. "I need you to support me on this. Help me keep things in perspective."

"Well." Resa picked up her purse. "Instead of worrying about treating diseased trees tomorrow or talking about Chase, let's drown our worries in cheeseburgers."

"And ice cream sundaes."

Focus on food. Focus on the dude ranch. Anything—other than Chase.

A massive backhoe contraption pulled a circular saw blade two and a half times as tall as a normal man. The teeth cut deep into the earth. The loud whirring made Chase's throat vibrate.

Dust swirled up from the ground. The air took on a cloudy haze, and he was glad Landry had insisted they wear surgical masks. As usual, she looked way too cute in hers.

He reached a hand out toward her. She hesitated, then clasped it as they stood side by side. A current moved up his arm. Shouldn't have touched her. But he needed her comfort, support, strength.

Please let this work, Lord.

The foreman pointed under a healthy tree. "See that grass wallowed down?"

"Yes." Was that a sign of oak wilt? *Not another diseased tree. Please.*

"You've got wild boar activity."

"Aren't they dangerous?" Landry shuddered, scanned the woods around them, as if they were being hunted.

"Don't worry, ma'am. The equipment will keep them away for today. But I wouldn't come out here alone or on foot just as a precaution." The foreman strolled back to his crew.

She dug her phone out of her pocket, tugged her hand from his, swiped the screen. She must have it on vibrate. Her eyes lit up.

A text? From Kyle? Frantic typing, then more swiping.

"Yes." She pumped her fist in the air, threw her arms around Chase.

Just where he didn't need her. In his arms.

He clasped her into a quick hug, then let go. As if she had no effect on him. As if his heart wasn't about to bust out of his chest.

"Devree has a wedding a week from Friday, but the couple's church basement flooded. Isn't that awesome?" She grimaced. "I mean, it's terrible. But they can't have the reception there, so Devree told them about us."

He frowned. "Just for the reception?"

"Maybe the wedding, too. I checked reservations on my phone. The date is open." She did a little bounce. "Devree said their style is rustic, so they should love the dude ranch."

"If I agree, that is." He blew out a breath. "Sounds like maybe we wouldn't have to flower the place up too much if they decided to have it here."

"You're such a guy." She rolled her eyes.

"I'll take that as a compliment." He refocused on the tree-saving equipment. "A local couple?"

"With local guests. We need to let them have it here. Their entire future is at stake. And if we don't, we'll be the dude ranch that ruined their lives. Word will get around."

"I'll think on it." He ignored her dramatics.

Getting ready for a wedding. Decorating. And keeping his distance from Landry. Could he really do this?

His gaze landed on the squashed grass at the base of the healthy tree. And an idea took shape. They might end up doing this wedding, but he had something to bring to the table, too.

Chapter Eleven

The morning spent researching gave Chase a stiff neck. But he had enough facts to back up the idea he'd had yesterday. He closed his browser. Then he grabbed his keys, locked his cabin, headed for the ranch house.

He opened the kitchen door. With her back toward him, Landry stirred something in a large mixing bowl, humming. Her favorite hymn—"The Old Rugged Cross." Her hair covered by her typical white shower cap.

Don't look at her. Just share the idea. Maybe since she was busy, she wouldn't even turn around.

"I have an idea."

She whirled around. The bowl slipped from her hands and bounced on the hardwood, spewing thick batter. It hit the corner of the cabinet door and shattered among globs of goo. Next to her bare feet.

"Don't move." He held his hands up.

"I'm fine—just get me some shoes."

"Why aren't you wearing any?" He tiptoed close.

"I bake better barefoot. And if you hadn't snuck

up on me, that cake would be in the oven instead of on the floor."

"All I did was come in the kitchen. I can't help if my nearness shakes you up." If only that were the case. He scooped her up.

"What are you doing?" She pushed against his chest.

"Rescuing a damsel in distress. I have to save those pretty little feet."

She rolled her eyes. "Put me down or you'll be in distress."

"Stop struggling or you'll make me drop you."

"Put me down."

"Shh. What will our guests think? I'm not putting you down with those bare feet until I get you out of the kitchen."

Her mouth clamped shut, and she stopped struggling. Her hands slid up his shoulders, fingers linked behind his neck. Lips close.

Stop looking. His heart couldn't afford another kiss. He shouldered the door open.

"Hello." She socked him in the shoulder. "Put me down."

Though his arms ached at the thought of letting her go, he complied.

She started for her private quarters.

"Hey, wait. Where are you going?"

"To get shoes. I have a mess in the kitchen and a cake to start over."

"I need to tell you my idea first."

"What?"

"A compromise. I'll agree to weddings here at the ranch if you'll agree to wild boar hunts. Hunters come from all over to hunt wild boar, and we'd be doing Texas a service since they're a menace."

"They tear up the land and they're dangerous." She crossed to the great room, settled in her favorite chair.

He followed. "Exactly."

"Wild boars only." She jabbed a finger at him. "Not deer."

"Boars only." He raised his right hand as if making a solemn vow.

"How will we keep trigger-happy hunters from going after the deer?"

"We'll set up hefty fines."

"But we can't have weddings with gunshots going off in the background."

"Guess you never heard of a shotgun wedding?"

Her eyes narrowed. "I'm serious."

"We'll schedule them around each other. The front part of the property and ranch house for weddings and guests. The back eighty for hunts. Maybe eventually, we could build cabins for the hunters."

"This could work." Her eyes lit up. "You're brilliant." She jumped up and hugged him.

And for two seconds, it was a celebratory friend hug. But then it hit him.

No more two-stepping around it. Chase had to

figure out a way to wrangle Landry's heart right out of Kyle's grip. The kiss had sealed it for him. He was in love with her. No denying it.

"I'd better get some shoes on and tackle the kitchen." She stood, went to her quarters.

"I'll meet you there." He had to up his game with her. No matter the toll her nearness took on his heart.

First on the agenda—they'd never gotten around to the second fishing trip she'd requested. Tomorrow. He'd figure out a way to make it happen.

"A-a-a-achoo." Landry covered her face with her hands.

"Bless you." Chase set down his tackle box. "You getting sick? Kind of sound stuffy."

"I think it's allergies." Why exactly had she suggested this fishing expedition? Because she hoped they could backtrack—back to easy camaraderie. But she was much too aware of Chase.

"Might be a summer cold. Maybe you should go back inside."

"I'm fine." She plopped down on the dock, kicked her shoes off and plunged her feet in the river. The water was cool and inviting in the heat.

"Keep your feet out of the water, you crazy woman." Chase settled beside her. The dock sank a bit with his weight.

"What fun is fishing if you can't dip your toes in the river?" She kicked her bare feet in the water.

Mostly to distract herself from him. Had she honestly thought going fishing would reverse how she felt about him?

"If you're sick, it'll make you sicker."

"That's an old wives' tale." She sneezed again.

"Just in case." He laid a towel across his knees, then grabbed her legs and hauled her feet out of the water and across his lap.

"Hey." But his proximity upset her pulse more than him manhandling her.

He wrapped the towel around her feet, patted them dry. "We don't need you catching pneumonia."

"True." Warmth spread through her. He cared. "Especially if we're about to get deluged with wild boar hunters. Any bites?"

"We have to get the news out first. I pick up the brochures and flyers we ordered next week, and I'll hang them up around town. You added both services on the website last night, so maybe we'll get nibbles soon. What about weddings?"

"The engaged couple can't align their schedules to come see our facilities until Monday. With so little time, they'll probably use us whether they like what they see or not. And our ad will be in the weekend edition of the newspaper." Their fishing poles lay forgotten on the dock.

This wasn't anything like their last fishing trip. Back before they'd kissed. When they'd actually cast their lines. But Landry didn't want to risk losing this closeness with him.

"Once we get the brochures and flyers," she said, "I'll give some to Resa and distribute them around town." The water lapped against the riverbank, and the call of birds echoed in the trees. But the peaceful surroundings couldn't calm the Chase-induced buzzing in her veins. "Maybe we should have an open house to advertise our new options."

"Great idea. We'll figure out a date and advertise. Ideally we'll get some takers soon."

Him approving her ideas warmed her heart. "One problem I came up with—will we have enough rooms for a corporate hunt?"

"I've done some research. Looks like most places accommodate eight hunters at a time."

"If we booked every room, we could sleep twenty-two men."

"You really don't want more than eight hunters at one time. So I think we'll be fine."

"Oh." She tried to push through the brain fog his nearness caused.

Over the last three weeks, they'd painstakingly built a tentative friendship. But now things could never go back to the way they were between them. Not for her, anyway. Landry had blown any hope of that when she'd allowed herself to fall for him.

"But I don't think we can handle large weddings." Chase plunked a white river rock in the water.

"Unless all of the wedding party lived locally." She should probably move her feet. But she didn't, enjoying his nearness. "We need to build some more cabins. Like yours."

"I don't think we need to take out a loan at this point."

"Agreed."

"Once we get some cash flow coming in, we can decide which service gets the most bookings, then decide whether to build cabins for weddings or the hunting ones we talked about. Eventually, ideally, we can do both."

"We'll start with local weddings or small out-of-town nuptials. Since a lot of the guests at a wedding will be married couples, we could easily sleep thirty-two." She blew out a breath. "But most couples plan weddings months in advance. So even if we get one booked, it'll be a while before it actually takes place. We need to decide on a deposit amount for saving our facilities for the designated date."

"We'll figure it out as we go." He patted her knee. "Will the weddings make you sad?"

"Maybe," she mumbled, closed her eyes, drawing in the comfort and strength of him. "But having Ally's wedding behind me helps. And Eden loved weddings. She'd love us hosting them here."

"You're right. She would." He gazed off across the lake. "If we're gonna fish, we need to get to it."

But she hated to move, to break the spell. "I guess I didn't really want to fish. I just needed to unwind a bit. I've been so keyed up over going home."

"Happy Trails" started up, and Chase leaned back to dig his cell out of his pocket.

"Hey, Mom. Sure. I'll be right there." He shoved her feet out of his lap, stood and pocketed his phone. "The McDougal family decided they're up for a trail ride." He picked up his rod. "You staying?"

"I'll be back in a bit. I have to cover the kitchen tonight so your folks can go to evening Bible study. But you can take my rod."

Spell broken. And a wave of loneliness hit her. As he walked away, she missed him. How could that be? When he was within shouting distance.

He was almost back to the main house, but his morning walk hadn't cleared Chase's head at all. Spending time with Landry was getting harder every day. Their non-fishing jaunt yesterday hadn't helped.

Hoofbeats echoed like thunder behind him. Coming closer. Chase turned around.

Landry emerged out of the wooded trail—still coming fast, like she might run him under.

"Whoa, slow down." The horse slowed as she

reined her in and stopped. Hooves danced with nervous energy. Finally the palomino settled, and Landry patted her shoulder.

"What was your hurry?"

"I didn't see you at first." Her cheeks reddened. She stroked Pearl's muzzle. "A morning ride seemed like a good idea. But I heard something. I never used to get creeped out in the woods. But now I know we have wild boars."

He ran his hand down Pearl's jaw, but Landry moved at the same time, and their fingers brushed.

All teasing went out of him. "Wild boars don't attack horses. And attacks on humans are rare. Usually during the mating season, which is November through January."

"Been studying up, huh?" Her eyebrow raised.

His ringtone started up. "Happy trails to you," Roy Rogers and Dale Evans crooned.

"We really need to get you a new ringtone." Landry grinned as she reined Pearl in the direction of the barn.

"I'm telling you, our guests like it." He dug his cell from his pocket, read the screen.

Paxton Miller, his brother-in-law. Were they still brothers-in-law with Eden gone? His hand shook.

"See you later." At least his feet still worked as he headed for the ranch house alone.

Paxton was a great guy. He'd loved Eden completely. They'd have had a long and happy marriage if she hadn't died. But thinking of Paxton always took Chase right back to the memory of his sister's last day. Her last minutes. Underwater. Struggling for air.

Stomach roiling, Chase made it to the house, stepped inside, crossed to the office. He settled in the rawhide chair, bent double, covered his face with his hands. Took several deep breaths as bile scalded the back of his throat. She was in Heaven now. No struggling or pain. He had to think of her that way. Beautiful Eden, happy and free.

His ringtone stopped.

A hand touched his back. "You okay?"

Landry.

A few more deep breaths. He sat up, faced her.

"What's wrong?" She knelt beside him. A worried frown marred her features as she took his hand in hers.

"That was Paxton."

Her face paled. Obviously Paxton's name gave her the same reaction. "Why did he call?"

"Don't know. I didn't answer. I'll call him. Just have to get my bearings first." He squeezed her hand. "It brings it all back."

"I know."

"I realize it was her idea to go scuba diving. That her tank was faulty. It was an accident. It wasn't Paxton's fault. He'd have saved her if he could. But thinking of him, somehow I don't think of their wedding. I think of her death."

"Me, too."

Of course she understood. Even though she hadn't been there when he'd gotten Paxton's frantic call, she'd lived the nightmare with him.

She stood, settled on his chair arm, wrapped her arms across his chest. "But let's think of her wedding. That gorgeous dress it took her a month of Saturdays to find. When she finally narrowed it down to two and then dragged you along to help her decide. The first time you saw her in it." Landry sniffled, and a tear dripped on his hand.

"How beautiful she looked at the church." His vision blurred. "How happy she was. Dad walking her down the aisle. Paxton couldn't take his eyes off her. He was the perfect man for my little sister. So good to her. Totally wrapped up in her."

"Better." She gave him a squeeze.

"Yes." He covered her hands with his, her long curls spilling down his chest.

"Want me to stick around while you call him?"

"Yes."

She pressed her cheek against his, but then she started to pull away.

He clamped tighter. "Right there. Stay right there while I make the call. I need extra strength." Or maybe he just needed her close. The silkiness of her cheek, the watermelon smell of her hair, the warmth of her embrace.

"I'll sit beside you, hold your hand once you dial." She let go of him but stayed on her perch.

His hand shook as he scrolled to recent calls,

tapped the number. It rang, and Landry twined her fingers with his.

"Hello?"

"Paxton. Sorry—I couldn't answer before." The truth.

"Chase. I'm glad you called back. Wasn't sure if you would."

"I—"

"It's just hard."

"Yeah."

"I know I should have kept in touch better." Paxton sighed. "But—"

"It's complicated."

"I guess we covered that. But I'm afraid I'm about to make it even tougher."

How could it get any more difficult? His little sister was dead. "What's going on?"

"I'm—I'm engaged."

It hit Chase like a kick in the gut.

Landry's grip tightened on his. She must have heard.

Paxton was moving on. Building a life with someone other than Eden. Some other woman would share his joys and sorrows, bear his children. While Chase would never have nieces and nephews.

"Oh. I see. I um…"

"I know. It's soon. But it's been almost a year."

"I know. I just…" Paxton deserved happiness.

Eden would want him to move on. Ten months. It seemed too soon. But who was Chase to judge?

"I'd like you to meet her. Your parents, too."

Landry squeezed his hand.

"I'm not sure…" What if they couldn't manage that? "You don't need our approval."

"I know. But I still love you guys. Still think of you as family."

"That means a lot." Chase swallowed hard. "We love you, too."

"How about tomorrow night? For supper."

"I'm not sure if—I can prepare Mom and Dad that quick."

"Just us for now. I mean, along with Savannah and anyone you'd like to bring. I can get with your folks later."

"Okay. I'll text you a place and directions."

"Thanks for agreeing. It's important to me, but I know…"

"It's tough."

"Yeah. See you tomorrow night."

Chase ended the call. "You heard?"

Her bleary gaze met his and she nodded, touched his face, wiped a tear he didn't realize had fallen. More followed.

Without a word, she understood his pain. Understood his heartbreak over Eden. How much he missed her. Because Landry felt it, too. She hugged him tight as he sobbed in her hair.

Chapter Twelve

Feeling shaky, Landry mustered a confident smile and squeezed Chase's hand as they stepped in the Old Spanish Trail Restaurant. She knew this place comforted him. Poor Chase. He looked like he could be sick any minute.

They both wanted Paxton to move on, to be happy. But they also wanted the one thing they could never have—Eden back.

The Friday night crowd was hopping, with only a few open tables.

In the John Wayne Room, Paxton sat in the corner with a delicate blonde. A play of emotions washed over his face—happiness, sadness—dread as he stood to greet them.

The two men hugged, clapping each other soundly on the back.

"It's good to see you." Chase sounded like he meant it.

"This is a pleasant surprise." Paxton gave Landry a quick hug, then reclaimed his seat and motioned to two empty chairs.

She and Chase settled across from the couple.

"This is my fiancée, Savannah." Paxton sucked in a deep breath. "My brother-in-law, Chase, and Eden's best friend, Landry. Landry is also Chase's partner in the dude ranch. And…?"

"We're friends." Their voices blended together.

"Friends who hold hands?" Paxton's eyebrows rose.

"On difficult days." Chase winced, and his gaze darted to Savannah. "I'm sorry. It really is nice to meet you."

"It's okay." Her chin-length hair framed a delicate beauty. "I understand completely." She turned to Paxton, devotion clear in her soft green eyes. "Paxton has told me so much about Eden. I wish I could have known her."

Landry's insides eased up. At least Savannah was willing to talk about Eden.

"Y'all were friends since culinary school?" Savannah sipped her water. "I wish I had a long-term friend like that."

I wish I had mine back.

Savannah frowned as she realized her mistake. "I'm so sorry."

"It's okay." Landry realigned her silverware. "I'm just glad I had her as long as I did."

The server stopped at their table, and they placed their drink orders.

The silence turned uncomfortable.

Until Savannah laughed. "Paxton had me in

stitches on the way here, telling me stories Eden shared about y'all."

"Really?" Chase lifted one brow.

"Stuff she told me." Paxton shrugged. "Mostly fishing trips."

"She always wanted me to take her." Chase's grin was real. "But she squealed and whined until I did everything for her."

"Same here." Landry closed her eyes, holding the memories tight of chasing Eden with a worm. "She didn't catch many fish. But when she did, she'd scream, drop the pole and run."

"I'd charge over and grab it just before the fish took off with it." Chase shook his head. "I really never understood why she wanted to go."

"With me, it was simply because she knew I loved it." Landry bumped her shoulder against his. "With you, because she wanted to hang out with her big brother. She worshipped you."

"It was mutual." Chase's gaze went distant. "We were a team. Never fought or argued like most siblings." He cleared his throat, focused on Savannah. "I'm sorry—I'm sure you don't want to talk about my sister all evening."

"I don't mind." Savannah faced Paxton. "Eden loved Paxton—she made him happy. I'm fine with her memory."

Paxton grinned at Landry and Chase. "It sounds like the two of you should go fishing together."

"We have." Their voices blended.

Chase's warm gaze landed on her. "Landry here—no qualms—baited her own hook, whether we used worms or the stinky stuff. Took her hook out of the fish she caught, even when they swallowed it. Even offered to clean our catch. If not for all those pesky FDA rules on commercial processing, I'd have let her."

Landry's insides melted at his approval.

The server came back with a drink-laden tray, and they placed their orders.

"Tell us how y'all met." Though Landry loved reminiscing about Eden, it really wasn't fair to Savannah.

"We went to high school together, but I was a few years younger, so we never dated or anything." Savannah tugged her gaze away from Paxton. "I went away to college. But last year, I came home, got a job teaching kindergarten at our old school. The heater went out in my classroom." Savannah's eyes bounced back to Paxton. "And the sweetest, cutest repairman I'd ever seen showed up to fix it."

Color crept up Paxton's throat. "My company services her school."

"He saved the day and my students."

"And asked you out?" Landry prompted.

"No." Paxton took Savannah's hand in his. "I wasn't ready."

"We struck up a friendship." Savannah fiddled with her earring, her voice soft.

"I confess, I changed her filters more often than

required." Paxton smirked. "But I didn't charge the school."

"He always stopped by right after the final bell rang, when my students were gone. Most of the time, he didn't even look at my heater. We'd just visit."

"Until I finally felt ready."

Landry glanced at Chase, his gaze riveted on the table. So quiet. At least he seemed less strained.

"Once he told me about Eden, I understood his caution." Savannah only had eyes for Paxton. "But I'm really glad he's prepared to move forward."

"Me, too." Paxton put his arm around her shoulders. "I know it seems fast. But things just developed."

"It'll be a long engagement." Savannah snuggled against his side. "There's no rush."

The server delivered their food.

Paxton held his hands out, and the foursome bowed their heads as he prayed. "Thank you, Lord, for this family, for allowing us to reconnect tonight, for bringing two wonderful women into my life, for this food and for all the blessings you give us. Amen."

Amens echoed.

"I hope you'll both come to the wedding." He focused on Chase. "Your parents, too."

Chase cleared his throat. "When?"

"Spring. April tenth."

"I'm sure Landry and I will come, and I'll check

with Mom and Dad." Yet Landry heard the strain behind his consent.

"There's something I want you to think about," Paxton said. "And if you don't want to, I'll understand."

"What?"

"I'd like you to be my best man."

Chase closed his eyes, nodded. "I'll think on it."

"Good."

When they got back to the dude ranch, Landry would be on double duty. Soothing Chase. A mix of torture and delight. But even more daunting— helping him figure out a way to break the news of Paxton's engagement to his parents.

The waning evening sun highlighted the feathery-leafed cypress trees lining the river, their knobby roots thick and strong. Water rippled over the surface in the cooling breeze, lapping at the white rocks lining the shore. Soothing, peaceful with the sway of the dock beneath him. But not enough. Chase wouldn't sleep tonight.

After arriving back from dinner with Paxton, he'd managed to escape Landry. Her arms—that made him long for her love and not just her comfort.

How would he break the news to his parents about Paxton's engagement? If only Paxton had never called. Just quietly gotten married without opening old wounds.

Yet exploring past hurts was sometimes part of the healing process. Chase loved Paxton. His folks did, too. They all wanted him to be happy. And Savannah seemed great. Like she and Eden could have been friends if they'd known each other.

Approaching footfalls sounded behind him. Landry coming to check on him. He couldn't handle her closeness. Her comfort when he was so vulnerable.

"There you are. I was worried. Don't you know how to answer your phone?"

"I left it in my cabin. But no need to worry. I'm fine."

On the dock now. Getting close.

"Are you really okay?" She plopped down beside him.

Way too close. "Just trying to figure out how to tell Mom and Dad."

"Want me to go with you?"

"Definitely." Couldn't help himself leaning into her.

"There's no way to ease into it. You'll just have to say it. It'll be hard on them. But they love Paxton. They'll want him to be happy." She picked up a nice, flat rock, hurled it across the water. It skipped four—five times.

"I just wish he'd waited a little longer."

"It seems like men remarry quicker than women. They don't do as well without a spouse after they've had one." She patted his hand. "Maybe don't rush this dinner. Let your folks get used to the idea. It helps that Savannah's really sweet."

"Yeah." He couldn't form another thought. Not while leaning against her, breathing her perfume. Her watermelon-scented hair.

"I think Eden would have liked her," Landry said.

"Yeah."

"Remember how Eden couldn't skip rocks?"

Laughter bubbled up his throat. "I tried to teach her, but she just chucked hers, and they plopped in the water like bombs."

"I tried, too. She got so frustrated." Landry giggled. "She swore I was keeping some secret technique from her."

"The harder she tried—" he closed his eyes and he could almost see her, his sweet sister plunking rocks like cannon balls "—the worse she got."

"And the madder she got."

"I thought she was gonna start chucking rocks at me." He guffawed.

"I tried to show her." Landry made the appropriate movement with her hand. "It's all in the wrist."

"But she got even madder because I couldn't stop laughing." He chortled as tears slid down his cheeks. "I miss her. So much."

Her arms slipped around his shoulders, and she pressed her face into his neck as her giggles melted into tears, too. Hugging and sobbing and sniffling together.

For as long as she'd been here, they'd mostly avoided the topic of Eden. Because he knew he'd crack wide open.

As his quaking subsided, they quieted.

And her nearness hit him full force. He pressed his lips against her temple.

She stilled—didn't even breathe. Then pulled away from him enough to catch his gaze. Confusion clear in her moist eyes.

"Chase?" His name came out a question.

A question he had to answer. He cupped her face, drew her to him until her lashes fluttered down. Their lips met. He tasted the salt on hers.

Her arms slid around his neck, and he felt like she was coming home.

But who was he kidding? She was still stuck on Kyle.

He pulled away. "I'm sorry." He stood, turned his back on her, strode up the deck away from her. Though his knees would barely hold him up. "I'm sorry. I'm sorry."

"Please stop saying that." Her voice caught. "It's kind of insulting."

"I got caught up—in memories—in grief—in comfort."

"We both did." The dock creaked as she stood, brushed off her jeans.

"It won't happen again." He ran his hand through his hair.

"It can't."

Because her heart still belonged to someone else. A man she obviously couldn't get over.

He had to think about his parents now. Not Landry. "You up for talking to my folks about Paxton?"

"Now?" Her tone incredulous.

"I'd like to get it over with." And he had to focus on something besides her.

"Sure. Just let me freshen up a little. Crying does a number on my fair skin."

He chanced a look at her. Nose and cheeks red. Lips redder.

She did a number on him.

She strode past him, completely natural. But then she bolted down the trail as if Bigfoot were real and after her.

Once she got out of sight, he sank back to the dock, unsure if his legs would get him to the ranch house. Breathing deep, her flowery perfume lingered.

Wow. He'd never felt sparks like that. Even more than during their pretend kiss.

But he didn't want what was left of Landry's shattered heart. He wanted all of it.

Blue Ajax swirls lined the inside of the tub. Landry's brain zinged faster than she could scrub. Why had Chase kissed her last night? Had it really been only grief and comfort for him?

Did he believe that was all it had been for her?

But Landry couldn't hide in the bathroom any longer. The fixtures sparkled, and their dinner guests would arrive soon.

Paxton's news had been hard on Janice and Elliot. But they'd adjusted and agreed to dinner with Paxton and Savannah tonight at the ranch house. The staff could handle their other guests for the evening.

The water turned a faint, cloudy blue as she rinsed until it ran clear down the drain. She scanned the bathroom once more, pulled off her gloves and washed her hands. Satisfied, she gave the bedroom one last survey.

The Rest a Spell Room had always lived up to its name. But the new soft suede bedspread with a scene in the middle of a cowboy kneeling at the cross, his horse behind him, added to the serenity. She could use some of that. She sucked in a big breath, then hurried out.

And almost ran into Chase. She hit the brakes.

"Whoa." But terrycloth scattered as he made an abrupt halt, then stooped to retrieve his load.

"Sorry." Trying not to look at him, she squatted to help.

"I saw a note the room needed fresh towels." Mess retrieved, he offered a hand to help her up.

She hesitated. Surely it wouldn't cause sparks to take his offer. She set her hand in his. But it did cause sparks. Enough to light up all of Texas. She couldn't afford to touch him, no matter how innocently. Not after last night on the dock.

"I already brought a fresh set up." She reached for the towels. "Let me have these. I'll take them to the laundry."

"I've got them." He turned toward the stairs, then waited until she descended first.

Chase hurried to drop off his load as Landry stashed her cleaning supplies in the closet. Just as he came back, Savannah stepped inside with Paxton following.

"Hey, y'all, glad you could make it." Landry tried for perky to cover Chase's unease.

"I felt odd just walking in." Savannah smiled. "But Paxton laughed at me when I started to knock."

"Fortunately, I stopped her." Paxton put his arm around her waist.

"This place is awesome." Savannah spun in a circle in the foyer, looking up at the massive beams of the gabled ceiling. "We should get married here."

She stopped spinning, clamped a hand over her mouth.

Chase's jaw clenched.

"It's okay—they're still in the kitchen." Landry touched her elbow. The dude ranch was open for weddings now. But not necessarily Eden's husband's.

"I've always loved this place." Paxton shoved

his hands in his pockets. "But I want our wedding to be somewhere that's ours."

"Oh, right." Savannah grimaced. "I forgot you and Eden got married here. Planned to live here. My brain-to-mouth filter doesn't function when I'm nervous."

"No need to be nervous." Chase's voice cracked. "Have a seat."

Landry wanted to give him a hug. But that was no longer an option. A hug might lead to something else. Something neither of them could handle.

Paxton settled on the couch with Savannah beside him. Landry sank into a cowhide wingback facing them. Chase chose the matching one on the other side of the massive fireplace.

"So, are there guests here?" Savannah glanced toward the stairway.

"At the moment we have only one room available." Her hands probably still smelled like Ajax from cleaning. "Weekends are usually our busiest time."

"I've never known anyone who owned a dude ranch or a hotel or anything. I'm just curious how it all works."

"Usually on Saturday night, Janice, Elliot and I would be working the kitchen. But all of our guests decided to go out tonight."

"It's like God arranged this evening for us." Savannah squeezed Paxton's hand.

Landry glanced at Chase. Stoic and silent.

Footfalls and voices in the foyer.

"I think Mom and Dad are coming." Chase cleared his throat, stood and hurried to greet them.

"I hate putting them through this." Savannah pursed her lips. "I know it's hard on them."

"It is." Landry shrugged. "But we all think the world of Paxton. And we're glad he found you. That he's happy again."

Whispers in the foyer, and several minutes passed.

Janice stepped into the room with Elliot close behind. Her chin quivered, and she pressed her fingers to her lips. Elliot gripped her shoulders.

Paxton stood with uncertain hesitation as Chase hovered in the doorway, while Landry tried not to cry and poor Savannah twisted the edge of her skirt into a knot.

"Oh, Paxton." Janice hurried to him and cupped his face in her hands as tears traced down her cheeks. "It's so good to see you."

"I'm glad." He bit his lip. "I wasn't sure how…"

"Of course we want to see you." Janice hugged him. "You made our little girl's last years—last days—the happiest of her life. I told myself I wouldn't cry."

Landry swiped a tear and glanced at Savannah. She was sitting alone on the couch, looking completely lost, yet she managed a tremulous smile.

Finally Janice let go of Paxton, and Elliot took her place. "Good seeing you, son."

As the hugging ended, Paxton reclaimed his seat next to Savannah. "I'd like you to meet my fiancée, Savannah."

"Sorry about all the tears." Janice dabbed her eyes, perched next to Savannah, patted the younger woman's arm. "We're very pleased to meet you."

"It's okay." Savannah's smile turned more confident. "I'm glad to see how much y'all love Paxton."

"Like Janice said, he loved our little girl." Elliot frowned. "Sorry."

"It's fine." Savannah wiped a tear. "I'm glad Eden was loved. She was a wonderful person from everything I've heard."

"Oh, dear, you're such a sweetheart." Janice handed her a tissue.

A buzzer went off.

"That's the oven." Landry jumped up, grateful for the excuse to escape the swirling emotion, and bolted for the kitchen.

Janice and Savannah came to help. Within minutes, they trooped to the table, each holding a dish and Landry settled beside Chase.

"It's like a family gathering." Janice took her seat at the end of the table. "With a few new members."

Silence filled the office. Mom and Dad's ease with Paxton last night was such a relief. But

Chase's heart wouldn't settle with Landry so near. He could separate his life into two categories—before the real kiss and after real the kiss.

They'd attended services together this morning. There was nothing like worshipping God with the woman you loved. If only she loved him back.

"Can you put the website password in for me?" She tucked her hair behind her ear. "With our engaged couple coming to see the ranch house tomorrow, I want to add how many we can accommodate for out-of-town wedding parties."

He stood, took a step. But he didn't want to get any closer. And besides, he knew her now.

"Better yet, I'll give it to you." He rattled off the code.

"Thanks." Her gaze latched on to his. A hand went to her heart. "It means a lot that you trust me with it."

Her cell phone buzzed, vibrating across the desk where she'd set it down.

She grabbed it, then frowned. "It's Kyle."

His breathing stopped. He'd expected it. But it had been over a week since news of his breakup, with no contact from him. He'd started to hope Kyle would stay out of the picture.

The phone buzzed in her hand. She just stared at it.

"You don't have to answer."

She met his gaze, as if she'd forgotten he was

there. "It won't hurt to see what he wants." She pressed a finger to the screen. "Hello?"

Stomach churning, he wouldn't stand here and listen while Kyle spun her back into his web. He couldn't. He made his escape as fast as his wobbly legs would carry him. Needing a break, he headed straight for his cabin.

But as he stepped out on the front porch, he noticed a figure on the porch swing. "Hey, Dad."

"What's got you down in the mouth?"

He leaned a hand against a log column, stared at the wooden floor of the porch. "She's on the phone with Kyle."

"Have you told her you love her yet?" Dad gestured to the seat beside him.

Chase settled in, propped his elbows on his knees, dropped his face in his hands. "Who said I did?" At the moment, he wished he didn't.

"So you're all tied in knots for the fun of it?"

"I can't stand to sit by and watch him hurt her again. That's all."

"Because you love her. You miss her when you're not with her. You worry about her. You love talking to her, spending time with her—even more than fishing, hunting or riding horses."

"It doesn't matter." He sat up, gripped the chain, the links pressing into his palm. "She's in love with someone else."

"You sure about that? I think she's done with

him. And even if she's not, he left her at the altar and moved on to someone else."

"He's not engaged anymore. Why do you think he called her?" His voice cracked. "But even if she's not interested in him, I don't want her on the rebound. I want her to love me." *Not to need me or offer me what's left of her heart after Kyle trampled it.* "She's not ready."

"Or maybe you're just scared."

"Of what?" Of her not feeling the same way. Of it not working out, but owning a business together. Of Kyle trying to come between them.

"Son, sometimes you have to take a chance. And sometimes taking chances hurts. But if you don't, you'll always regret it. Wonder what if. What might have been. Is that any way to live?"

"But what if she doesn't feel the same way?" His biggest fear. "Or she does, but we crash and burn?"

"Then you'll have to decide if you can go back to being her friend. Maybe the two of you are supposed to be just friends. Or maybe you're meant to be more. But you'll never know unless you tell her how you feel."

"I never wanted this." He ran his hand through his hair. "I never wanted to own the dude ranch. I only want to handle the recreation stuff." He'd been content with that. Until Landry changed everything.

"She got in your heart. And everything changed." Dad twisted his wedding ring round and round. "That's what happened when I met your mom. I never wanted to own a restaurant. That was her dream."

"But you seem happy. I always thought it was your dream, too."

"As long as your mom's by my side, it is my dream. She handles the books. I get to cook. We're a great team." Dad leaned forward, patted his knee. "The right woman changes everything."

Was Landry the right woman? His heart sure insisted she was.

He just had to show her he was the right man for her. How could he convince her to give him a chance?

Landry held her breath as her sister, in wedding planner mode, showed her engaged couple around. The bride-to-be caught her fiancé's gaze and smiled.

That had to be good. Even though there were only four days until their wedding and the dude ranch was probably their only choice, she still wanted the couple to like what they saw.

"So, we could have the wedding here in the great room?"

"Your guest list is relatively small. We'll have plenty of room," Devree said. "We'll move all the furniture out. Imagine coming down that staircase, then saying your I do's in front of the fireplace."

"What do you think, honey?" The groom, eager to please.

"I really like it."

"Me, too." Relief tinged his tone. Over the rustic setting or that a decision had been made?

Landry squelched a sigh. There was no way the groom could feel half as relieved as she did. She needed her idea for hosting weddings to be successful. To prove her worth to Chase? Like it would make any difference.

"Having the wedding and reception in one place makes it easier on everyone involved." Devree cinched the deal. "And more people will stay for the reception if they don't have to change locations."

"If more people stay, will we have enough food?" The bride's hand went to her heart.

"Landry is a chef, the restaurant here caters and there's a second chef on staff. For an extra fee, they'll handle overflow."

"But it's already Monday. The wedding is Friday evening."

"Not a problem." Landry handed the jittery bride a brochure of the restaurant's catering services.

"Oh, Devree, what would I do without you?" The bride flipped through the glossy package descriptions and didn't even blink at the prices. "You think of everything." Her hand stilled. "Where will I get ready for the ceremony?"

"There are a variety of rooms with ample space upstairs," Landry said. "We'll provide one." All this info was in the new dude ranch brochures Chase had gone to pick up from the printer.

"We'll have to call the florist, the bakery, the guests and who knows who else to tell them about the change."

"Relax." Devree put a comforting hand on the bride's shoulder. "I'll take care of the vendors. And if you'll compile a contact list, I'll get in touch with your guests, also."

The door opened, and when Landry saw Chase walk in, she stopped breathing for a moment.

"Oh, good, here's Chase with more brochures." Devree met him at the door. "Now we can make some final decisions."

"Hot off the presses." He set a box on the reservation counter, slit it open with a letter opener.

"Perfect timing." Landry sorted through them, then handed the bride one of each. "Chase, this is Missy and Victor. They've decided to have their wedding and reception here Friday night."

"Nice to meet you." Chase shook hands with the groom.

"We appreciate you accommodating us on such short notice." Missy giggled, the typical giddy bride. "Not just any man would put up with an instant wedding." She grinned at Landry. "You must have a very special husband."

"We're not married." Landry's words blended with Chase's.

The bride's mouth formed a small O.

"We're business partners. Chase lives in a cabin on the property." Landry didn't want anyone thinking there was impropriety going on.

"I'll let y'all get back to wedding planning." His mouth seemed to have tipped down after her explanation. "I've got lots of work to do." He hurried out of the room.

He'd been odd since the kiss. Worse since Kyle had called about possibly booking his client a hog hunt. She probably should have explained, but she didn't want to get his hopes up for nothing.

Maybe he was just eager to get busy with the fencing for the hog hunts. Exhausting work and now he'd spend part of his upcoming days moving furniture and getting ready for the wedding. He hadn't signed up for either. His plan had been to lead trail rides and host camping and fishing trips. None of which was work to him.

Was he tired of the dude ranch? It had never been his dream. It had been Eden's. He'd only signed on to help after Granny's death. But now that she couldn't imagine her life without him, was Chase wanting out?

Chapter Thirteen

The sturdy field fencing dug into Chases' gloved hands as he stapled it onto the post. Wedding planning had kept Landry busy yesterday, but this morning he couldn't shake her.

"Even though the boars will be fenced in, don't we need to hire a guide?" She pushed the roll along the barren ground, uncoiling enough length to reach the next post. "Maybe wait and hire one if we get a hunt booked?"

"I worked as a guide on a ranch back when I was traveling. And you'll never guess what Ron's job was before they moved here. A hunting guide at an exotic ranch in San Angelo."

"No way. It's like God orchestrated the whole thing for us."

"He did." If only God would help him make Landry fall in love with him.

"Is it really hunting if the boars are fenced in and we feed them corn?"

Chase chuckled. "It's the only way to guarantee hunters will see action. Trust me, this is how all the hunting ranches do it. We're trying to appeal to business executives with limited time. They don't want to spend days tracking and trailing. They're out to make memories and end up with meat in their freezers."

He clamped the fence stretching tool on the woven fencing, and she helped him tug it tight to the next post.

"So they really can jump any fence shorter than this?"

"According to the ranch where I worked and my research, up to three feet. This one is four."

Her phone rang. She tugged off her work glove and dug the phone from her pocket. Her eyes widened. He'd seen that look before.

"Him again?"

She nodded.

"Don't answer it." Chase gritted his teeth.

"I have to." She swiped her finger across the screen. "Hello."

He could hear a male voice but couldn't make out what Kyle was saying.

Chase tried to concentrate on the fence. But he couldn't get past the fact that the woman he loved was on the phone with the man *she* loved. The man she'd almost married. Would have married if left up to her.

"That's awesome. I can't tell you how grateful we are. Yes, text me the number."

Now he was texting her?

He missed the nail and nicked his thumb instead. "Ouch." He gritted his teeth against the throbbing.

He saw Landry wince on his behalf. "Thank you so much," she said into the phone, then listened for several minutes as her gaze met his. "Yes. I'll call him ASAP. Thanks." She ended the call. "Are you hurt?"

"It's fine." His thumb was still throbbing.

"Let me see." She grabbed his hand, tugged his glove off, inspected his thumb. Her tender caring lighting him up like a starry sky on a clear Texas night.

He pulled his hand away, stuck his glove back on.

The suspense might kill him, but at least her conversation with Kyle hadn't sounded romantic. Yet.

"One of his father's business associates is interested in a corporate hog hunt for eight men next weekend. Kyle saw our ad, and he's been talking us up. He's texting me the man's number."

"No!" Chase jerked the fencing into place and hammered a nail in with one blow. Thankfully none of his digits got in the way. "Absolutely not. I will not guide that good-for-nothing on a hunt."

She laughed. While his insides boiled.

"Kyle's not coming. Can you imagine him hunting?"

"Of course not. What was I thinking? He might get blood on his wingtip shoes. But why not just have the associate call us?" Because Kyle wanted to talk to Landry. To reel her in again. Maybe Chase would bow out. Let Kyle have her.

"He's just doing a little legwork for his client to get in his good graces."

"I think that's enough fencing for the day." Chase started gathering tools.

"But there's still plenty of daylight left."

"I'm done." His tone came out harsher than he'd intended.

Wordlessly she dropped the pliers in his toolbox.

They mounted their horses, headed back to the house. After they arrived, he'd slip away to his cabin, make a call and set up a meeting.

Though he was tempted to give up. Walk away. He would not stand by and watch her get mixed up with Kyle again. One thing was certain. He could not stay here and pine over her while she pined over another man.

Before Landry ever looked up from the reservation counter, she knew the footfalls coming from the kitchen were Chase's. Back from Wednesday night Bible study. Hadn't seen him since their fencing jaunt yesterday. She gave him a bright smile when he came into view.

One he did not reciprocate. Stiff and scowling, like the day she'd arrived.

"I need to go out of town Saturday for a short meeting." He wouldn't even look at her.

"Oh." Was he still sore over her taking Kyle's call? Was he jealous? No. He just didn't like Kyle. She waited for an explanation.

Nothing. Without another word, he turned toward the door and left her standing there.

The phone rang and she jumped. Resa's number.

"Hey, Resa. Sorry I never called you to set up another lunch." *I have to stay around here and moon over Chase.*

"No worries. So, any new developments on the Chase front?"

She leaned her elbows on the counter. "I wish I could say life has gotten back to normal. But things have been strained." Especially since their kiss on the dock. But she hadn't told Resa about that.

"What's wrong?"

"We're uncomfortable around each other. And he's going off on some mysterious trip Saturday."

"That's what happens when friends kiss and sparks fly." Resa's voice went soft. "Things get awkward and mysterious."

"I think you should tell me about your *friend.*"

"Nothing to talk about. It was a long time ago." Resa sighed. "But speaking of times gone by, my folks' anniversary is coming up next spring— thirty years."

"Oh, wow, that's awesome."

"Dad told me this afternoon he wants to surprise Mom with a vow renewal ceremony where they originally got married."

"At the dude ranch. That's so sweet." Landry pulled up the calendar. "What month?"

"May. I hope you're not already booked up."

"I wish we had bookings that far out. Our advertising campaign hasn't kicked into high gear yet."

"Oh, good. He'll be so excited." Resa's smile echoed in the lilt of her voice. "Can you give me Devree's number? I know I won't have time to pull this thing together."

"Sure. I'll text it to you."

"Mom will love it." Resa's tone turned animated. "I'll have to think of a way to get her there. Maybe just that I want them to see the place with our furniture in it."

"That would work."

"I can't wait to see her face."

"If you could get me some pictures of the original wedding, we could try to recreate the setting."

"Great idea. Oh, Landry, thanks so much. This will mean the world to Mom and Dad."

"I'm thrilled to help."

"I didn't even ask you about the price."

"It's on me."

"No. It absolutely is not. You're trying to build up business, and besides, Chase bought a ton of furniture last year and I've gotten a couple of orders from your guests lately. I'm definitely paying you. I'll get one of your pricing brochures from Devree."

"Oh. All right. Just be that way." Resa could

afford it, but Landry hated to think of charging her friend.

"I hope Devree is available. Thanks for everything. I'll talk to you soon."

As Landry hung up, the door opened and Chase stepped inside. "Another booking, I hope."

She relayed her conversation with Resa.

"I never really thought about renewal ceremonies."

"Me, neither, but it will open whole new income avenues." She picked up a box of lights. "I know it's not your idea of fun, but can you help me start decorating for the wedding Friday?"

"Sure. Let me have that." He took the load from her, carried it into the great room.

Tell me about your trip. Maybe if she prompted him, he'd share.

"How long do you think you'll be gone Saturday?" Her smile slipped.

"I'll be back that evening."

Her stomach sank. He'd be back. But he didn't say he'd stay.

Silence. Except for his footfalls.

She wanted to pepper him with questions. What was his trip about? Why wouldn't he tell her? How long before he left for good? Was he setting up the perfect opening to walk away?

Day two of wedding prep and Chase had hung more twinkle lights than he could ever count, along with burlap bows, and unpacked candleholders made from logs. But he didn't mind. The work kept his mind busy and off Landry and Kyle's call. Except she was in his workspace. He'd bumped into her twice as she tied burlap bows on chairs while he set them up.

"So I officially booked the corporate hunt for next weekend for Kyle's client." Landry fluffed a bow just so.

His stomach soured. "And you're certain he's not on the guest list."

"Even if Kyle wanted to hunt—" she rolled her eyes "—I wouldn't allow him to stay here."

Really? But Chase had a feeling her ex-fiancé could smooth-talk her into anything he wanted.

"I just hope you won't let your guard down with him. Remember how badly he hurt you. He's not worthy of you."

"Thanks." Her voice went soft.

Reeling him in even more than he already was.

"I'm so excited." She clapped her hands. "Are we ready for our first hunt?"

"I got most of the fencing up." But it was only a matter of time before Kyle showed up. Calling her, helping her business was just the beginning. Chase had to head him off.

"I can help you some more next week."

"Actually, Ron's helping me finish the fencing." Her hands halted over the bow she was fluffing. "I guess you weren't happy with the work I did."

"You were fine. But having two men, we'll get the job done faster, and your hands will heal." He ran his thumb over a scratch along the back of her hand, then jerked away. Shouldn't have touched her.

"I didn't mind. It's nice to get outside."

"No offense, but Ron is stronger."

"You're right." She finished the bow and stood. "Do you need any help with your meeting Saturday?"

His heart hammered. If she learned what he was up to, his whole plan might backfire. "I've got it under control."

And after his meeting, maybe the future would be clear for them. Landry needed someone new in her life. Someone who could make her forget Kyle. And Chase knew just the cowboy.

All the work they'd done over the last several days had been worth it. The bride's teary appreciation when she'd seen the great room was priceless. Along with the nice check Landry had handed Chase to put in the bank. Proof that Landry's ideas were viable. Proof that the dude ranch—and Chase—needed her.

As time for the ceremony neared and guests waited, Landry surveyed the decor. Twinkle lights lined the ceiling, burlap and red gingham ribbons flanked the chair backs, with tree stumps holding log candleholders lining the aisle as if the bride's decor had been chosen for this very setting.

Guests pointed, admiring the heavy beams lining the ceiling, the rockwork and fireplace. If only the rustic furnishings weren't crammed into her private quarters with barely room to walk through. But she'd given a few of the early guests a tour. Maybe they'd book rooms here in the future or tell their friends and family about it.

Chase ushered a few more guests inside, looking way too handsome in his customary Western jacket, jeans and boots. His blue shirt turned his normally green eyes the same shade.

"I think everyone's here," he whispered. "Devree said to go ahead and sit down. It's time to start." Not as stiff toward her as yesterday.

His hand settled at the small of her back. Certain her knees would buckle, she sat in the first chair she came to in the back row.

"You okay?" He claimed the seat beside her. "I know weddings are rough on you."

"I'm fine." She really wasn't. But it had nothing to do with memories.

The pianist began playing, and Landry was glad the Donovans had never parted with Granny's piano. The bridesmaids came downstairs and lined up in the entryway. As the music built, the first bridesmaid walked down the aisle. They kept coming until all the attendants had trailed inside and lined up on the left side of the fireplace.

The music changed to the wedding march, and the crowd stood and turned to face the doorway. Missy descended the stairs in a cloud of white, her smile wide enough to light the night sky outside. At the bottom of the staircase, her father offered his arm, then walked her to the altar and her waiting groom.

The look on the groom's face put an ache in Landry's heart. If only Chase would look at her that way. If only this were their wedding.

The preacher prayed over the couple. At his "Amen," the crowd sat. And the groom continued to gaze at his bride with love. He didn't lean close and whisper something. He didn't leave her standing there alone. When they got to the vows, he repeated them like he meant them.

She felt Chase's gaze and glanced up at him. He looked away. Probably thought she was upset about Kyle. But Kyle no longer had the power to upset her.

Chase did. And he was planning to leave her.

A short meeting. No matter how much she'd questioned him, he'd kept his trip mysterious. But she'd figured it out. The only reason he could be keeping this secret was that it involved her and their business partnership. He must be meeting with a potential manager for his half of the dude ranch.

The joy in scheduling his fourth wild boar hunt wouldn't settle inside Chase. He went through the motions of getting all the contact info, setting up the deposit and balance due. Enough to replace the funds they'd used for fencing supplies from their business account.

"That's everything I need. We'll see you September eighth, Mr. Norwood."

His plan was working. He should be happy, but all he could think about was making sure Kyle wouldn't move back into Landry's life. If today's meeting went as planned, maybe he could permanently remove the threat. Then Chase could woo Landry and patiently wait until her love for her ex cooled.

But it could backfire on him. She might learn what he was up to. If she didn't have any feelings for him, she might cut him out of her life instead of Kyle.

Landry stepped into the office.

Chase tried not to stare. Her ruffled orange skirt ended a few inches above her boots, topped off by a lacy white blouse and brown fringed jacket. Feminine and all cowgirl. If only she were *his* cowgirl.

"How come you're so dressed up? It's Saturday."

"Becca has a stomach bug, so I'm on hostess duty."

"I just booked another hog hunt."

"That's awesome." She approached, stopped in front of him. Her forehead scrunched. "But do you think we have enough hogs for all these hunters?"

"I scouted a sounder of twenty or so yesterday,

and I don't think they were the same ones I saw the day before."

"I guess a sounder is like a herd?"

"They usually travel in groups of one or more sows and their piglets. The boars keep to themselves unless they've got their eye on a sow. Kind of like cowboys." All the more reason for his trip.

"Or men in general." She hugged herself. "Look, I know you're not happy here."

"What makes you think that?" Did his trip have her worried? But he had to do this, and he couldn't tell her what it was about. Their future depended on it.

"You don't have to stay here for me." She shrugged. "And I'm not talking about buying you out—I mean, if you wanted to be a silent partner, I'd be fine with that."

Was she trying to get rid of him? To make way for Kyle to come back to her?

He had his truck tank full of gas. All Chase had to do was walk out the door. So why was it so hard to leave?

Because of Landry.

"You'll be okay while I'm gone?"

"Of course. I'll have plenty to keep me busy getting ready for our first hog hunt next weekend. I'll be fine."

But would he be okay without her?

It was just for a day. He had to make sure Kyle

stayed firmly in her past, so when he got back they could work toward the future. Ideally together.

"All right, then," he said. "Call if you need anything?"

Suddenly she rushed toward him. Her arms slid around his shoulders, face in his chest. He returned her embrace. Searing her into his heart. For the rest of time, he could stay right here, holding her. But he had to go. Had to tear himself away.

"I'll call when I get there." He stepped back. "Just to let you know I made it okay."

"Drive safe."

He turned away, one foot in front of the other and out the door.

Could he really do this? Even if today's meeting went like he hoped, could he live and work with her while he loved her and she loved Kyle? Was he strong enough to keep his feelings under wraps? And wait for her?

The elevator stopped on the twelfth floor. What kind of consulting service was open on Saturday? He'd expected to have to wait until Monday, been surprised when he'd called and gotten the appointment. Maybe it was a Dallas thing. But didn't most executives get the weekend off?

As Chase stepped into the plush lobby, the receptionist smiled.

"May I help you?" Perfect white teeth, her brunette hair cut short, too severe.

"I'm Chase Donovan. I have an appointment with Kyle Billings at three."

"Please have a seat. I'll tell him you're here."

While the receptionist made the call, Chase sank into a fancy clear chair with a silver frame that didn't look sturdy enough to hold him up.

He'd called Landry from the parking lot to let her know he'd made the drive safely. Their conversation had been stilted.

His heart clenched. This meeting had to go well.

Minutes passed, the clock ticking loud.

"Mr. Billings is ready to see you now." The secretary stood, ushered Chase to a heavy paneled door.

Kyle's hair was mussed. Dark circles around his bloodshot eyes.

"Are you drunk?"

"I wish." He waved Chase inside. "How much do you need?" Kyle pulled a checkbook out of the inside pocket of his jacket.

"I'm not here for your money."

Kyle's gaze met his. "I assumed you were looking for investors when you called. Then what?"

"I'm not stupid. I know you calling about the hog hunt was only a ruse to worm your way back into Landry's life."

"So you're here about Landry?"

"I want you to leave her alone." He jabbed his finger in Kyle's face. "You got that? You've hurt her enough."

"You're right. I have."

"So you'll leave her alone?"

"She doesn't love me." Kyle's eyes closed. "I'm not sure she ever did."

This was easier than Chase had expected. He took a step back. He'd half anticipated a fistfight. Or at least a war of words. But Kyle seemed so beaten.

"Do you still love her?"

"Not sure I ever did. I was on the rebound from Waverly when I met Landry." Kyle turned toward the window. "She just got caught in the cross fire. She's a wonderful woman, but not the woman for me."

"You love Waverly. Not Landry."

Kyle nodded. "You don't have to worry. I'm trying to win Waverly back." He sank to the edge of the upscale sofa, covered his face with his hands. "Besides, Landry loves you. That day in San Antonio—she never looked at me the way she looks at you."

But she'd only been pretending.

"Then we're done here." Chase cleared his throat. "If you have any more associates who want to book our ranch, don't call her. Have them call me."

"Trust me, she's not interested." Kyle raised his hands in surrender. "And I'm not, either."

Chase hurried out. On autopilot, he stepped in

the elevator, punched the ground-level button and inched his way down the skyscraper.

Eleven hours. What kind of meeting could take Chase so long?

She lay across her bed, still fully dressed, her insides aching with missing him. He had to come back. He had to stay. He just had to. She longed to press her ear to the door, even though she couldn't ever hear a thing from her soundproofed room.

After dealing with his absence for a mere day, she was convinced. She loved Chase. Missing him for a day had been torture. She'd never missed anyone so much. Not even her family.

A knock on her door had her bolting upright and clasping a hand to her heart. She stood, smoothed her hands over her rumpled blouse and skirt, hurried over and swung the door open.

Chase. His hat pulled low, cowboy gear unruffled, spicy cologne intact. A sight for a sore heart.

"You're back." Did the ache echo in her voice? It took everything she had to keep from hurling herself at him.

"I know it's late, but I saw your light. Are you up for a family meeting?"

"Sure." Family? Did he have news? Had he met with a potential manager?

"Mom and Dad will be here in a few minutes." He strolled into the great room, settled in a wingback by the fireplace. "Anything that needs my immediate attention?"

Me. "Everything ran smoothly." Great way to make him feel indispensable. "But you're always needed around here."

For once, couldn't he sit on the couch, so she could get closer to him without looking like an idiot? She perched in the other wingback. Twiddled her thumbs. Trying to keep her nerves from shooting off into orbit. She couldn't imagine him selling his share of the ranch, but maybe he'd met with the lawyer to sell her his half once their year was up.

In that case, how would she come up with the funds? But more importantly, would he leave? Go back to traveling? If so, there was more at stake. She couldn't lose Chase. Even though she couldn't have him. If he left, how would she function with half a heart?

Janice bustled in, fluffing her hair, but the lines her food prep hat left were too stubborn to be rubbed away. "So, what's this about, son?" Elliot wiped his brow with his sleeve. They settled on the couch.

"Paxton called me today."

Had Paxton changed his mind? Decided to keep his share of the dude ranch. Could he do that?

"Please tell me they don't want to do the wedding here." Janice linked her arm with her husband's. "I love him, and Savannah is so sweet, but I just don't think I'm up for that."

"That's not why he called." He let out a wobbly sigh. "The life insurance company concluded the investigation into Eden's accident."

Landry's heart tugged like it always did when she thought of Eden.

"They concluded—" he closed his eyes "—that her air tank was faulty. The payout is a substantial amount."

Landry gasped at the number he quoted. "That's a lot of money." Her eyes grew teary. "But she was worth more."

"She was." He cleared his throat. "He's sending the full amount in two checks to our business accounts. Half to the restaurant, half to the dude ranch."

"What?" Janice's hand flew to her heart. "Oh my goodness. Is he certain that's what he wants to do?"

"He says he doesn't need it, and Eden would want the money to go to the businesses."

Landry knew she would.

"It's the perfect gesture to honor Eden." Janice swiped under her eyes. "We'll have to call and thank him."

"So, that's where you went off to today?" Elliot handed Janice a tissue, put his arm around her.

"No." Chase ran a hand through his hair, set his

hat in place and stood. "Think I'll turn in. Traffic was crazy, and I'm exhausted."

Traffic where?

"We'll see you in the morning, Landry." Janice stood. Holding hands, she and Elliot left the room.

With the business account plumped u , they wouldn't have to work so hard. The dude ranch was firmly in the black. The business didn't need her as much. Didn't need Chase as much.

Had he known about Paxton's donation before today? Was he weaning her? Seeing if she could stand on her own so he could move on without her?

More importantly, how could she convince him they should both stay?

Chapter Fourteen

Landry stroked Pearl's velvety neck. The palomino shuddered as if she was keyed up, too. The horses usually soothed her, but nervous hoof stamping and whinnies filled the barn. Like they knew something was up.

This morning she'd gone to church. Tonight it was Chase's turn. In between services, they'd barely seen each other. Barely spoken, both busy making final preparations for tomorrow evening's open house. She missed him.

Footfalls thudded across the barn galley. A cowboy approached, tall, burly. Nash Porter. A shiver crawled up her spine. Out of all the ranch hands, he was the only one who made her nervous. She pressed herself against the barn wall, hidden by shadows. It wasn't that she was afraid of him. But there was something shady about the man.

He passed without noticing her.

"Hey, Nash." Chase coming up the path, fifty yards away. "Have you seen Landry? Dad said he thought she came out here."

"No, sir. But I wouldn't have mind…" Nash's words stalled as if he remembered he was talking to his boss.

"You were saying?" Chase's tone hardened.

"Let's just say your little plan can't be too hard with her being such a looker."

"What plan?"

Landry peered through the shadows at the two men bathed in moonlight in front of the barn.

"I've been on to you awhile." Nash spit a stream of tobacco in the dust. "It's been fun to watch."

"I'm not sure what you're talking about."

"I know what you're up to. She's sweet on you, and you're working it so you can keep the ranch in the family. I gotta hand it to you. Marry her, trick her into to signing anything you want her to."

A horse whinnied and Landry edged along the wall to the back door, then shot to the cover of trees. Farther into the woods, she stayed hidden and bolted past them toward the ranch house. They'd probably hear her, but figure it was only a deer.

Why hadn't she seen it? All the mixed signals. The stolen kisses. It all made sense now. Chase was playing her. Her stomach twisted. And with the suddenly large business account, he had even more at stake. Maybe he'd known all along that the large sum was coming.

He didn't feel a thing for her and had only been

charming her in order to get her half of the dude ranch. And she'd fallen for it.

Her vision clouded. How could she be so stupid? How could he be so heartless?

She couldn't stay here. She had to pack her bags and get away. First thing in the morning, she'd slip out, drive to town to see the lawyer, arrange to sell her share to Chase and go home. The place she'd never expected to return to. Heartbroken and betrayed all over again.

Thanks to Chase's performance at Ally's wedding, everyone in Aubrey thought she had a new boyfriend. Once she arrived home single, she'd be labeled a failure again. This time, though, she'd make sure everyone knew *she* was the one who'd broken things off. Technically true, since she was the one bailing on his plan.

If only she didn't have to face his parents—but she had to let them know she wouldn't be around.

She stepped up on the back porch, straightened her spine, tried for casual as she entered. Elliot and Janice were bent over the counters, deep in food preparation as usual.

"Did Chase find you?" Janice's paring knife made quick work of a potato.

"No. Can y'all manage without me tomorrow?" And from now on. But she'd break the news after she'd seen the lawyer.

Janice gasped. "Tomorrow's our open house."

How could she have forgotten? "Sorry. I meant the day after tomorrow."

"Oh." Janice relaxed.

"Sure." Elliot shot her a wink. "Not that we don't need you around here. But if you have something else you need to do, we'll be fine."

Always so kind to her. Both of them.

"I have to run some errands. I probably won't be back until late afternoon."

Janice never looked up. "Need Chase to go with you?"

The air went out of her lungs. "No. I'll be fine."

She'd miss them. Miss talking and working with them. She sucked in a shuddery breath and headed for the foyer.

The back door opened. Chase. "There you are."

Why hadn't she kept moving? Made it to her quarters before he returned.

He held her gaze for excruciating moments, then turned to his dad. "I need you to back me up in the office. I'm firing Nash Porter."

To keep him quiet?

"I'm so relieved." Mom wiped her brow with the back of her wrist. "I don't like the way he leers at our guests, or our staff, for that matter."

Landry inched toward the exit.

"Wait." Chase eased up next to her as if she were a skittish colt. "When I get finished with this, can we talk?"

"Another time." Did he suspect she'd overheard?

"I'm turning in early, resting up for our open house tomorrow. And I have errands to run the next day."

"We seem to be going in different directions lately." Was that regret in his tone? Did he at least like her? Regret manipulating her? Or was it an act?

Her mouth tightened. "I have to go." She headed for the door while her legs would still carry her. Leaving him standing there with a puzzled look on his face. He obviously had no clue she was on to him.

But she knew he didn't really care. And he wouldn't play her. No man would, ever again.

Their open house was underway, but Chase wasn't so sure he could pull off Landry's vision for the event. They had tons of finger foods and plenty of brochures with a good fifty guests milling about. But he had one very beautiful distraction to contend with.

"Ready?" Chase raised his eyebrows.

"I hope so." Landry stepped away from him. Why was she so stiff today? Just nervous?

He clinked a large spoon against a glass. Conversations faded, and their guests faced them.

"Hello." Landry cleared her throat. "We're so glad y'all decided to visit with us today. Our goal is to make you feel at home."

"As you'll notice—" Chase adjusted his hat

"—the trough is overflowing. Feel free to go back for seconds and we'll split up into groups. If you're interested in the horses, Earl and Levi will take you out to the barn," he said, pointing toward the two ranch hands. "If you're interested in wild boar hunts, Ron, Troy and I will take you to the back eighty."

Landry put on her best smile, but somehow it didn't reach her eyes. "For a tour of the rooms, Becca and Janice will show you around. Or if you'd like to have a wedding here, my sister, Devree, and I will walk you through our facilities."

"If you're interested in more than one tour—" Chase shoved his hands in his pockets "—no worries. We'll swap around when we all return."

The guests broke up, then regathered in groups around the respective leaders. An equal number seemed interested in weddings and hunts. Proving both their ideas were spot on. That they were a great team.

"This was such a brilliant idea," he murmured against her ear.

Her cheeks turned pink.

And her nearness went right to his head—clouding his common sense.

She sidestepped away from him.

Huh? Maybe she was keeping her distance for their guests. To keep any notions of impropriety at bay. He had to pull it together. Had to stay focused.

"You ready?" Devree whispered, turned a smile on their guests.

"Sure." But Landry didn't sound like her heart was in it. What was with her? The open house was her idea.

"Okay, let's talk weddings." Devree led the group of a dozen or so into the great room, with Landry trailing behind.

Chase wanted to follow, but the thought was quickly dashed.

"We've got a dozen interested in hunts." Ron shot him a what's-your-hold-up look. "You ready?"

What could he say? *"Um, nah, I'd rather go on the wedding tour"*?

"Of course." Chase turned to the guests. "Follow me for wild boar hunts." He led the gathering out the exit. "We've got three trucks, so let's split up."

The tour guides each went to one of the vehicles. Chase climbed in his truck and waited for his passengers.

Why was Landry giving him the cold shoulder? Somehow he knew it had to do with something more than their guests.

The aged rockwork on the outside of the lawyer's office went right along with the interior. It was a whitewashed farmhouse with plank floors and walls. There were aged barn wood door facings and trim work, with vintage furnishings.

Trying not to think about Chase, Landry flipped through a magazine while waiting. Yesterday's open house had been a roaring success. Even more so since she'd been able to avoid Chase all day, then slip away to her room after helping his parents clean the kitchen.

"Mr. Abbott can see you now."

"Thank you." Landry set the magazine down, and the middle-aged secretary, slim and fashionable, ushered her to a paneled door.

"Ms. Malone, how nice to see you." Mr. Abbott gestured to the wingback across from his massive cherry desk.

"I'm sorry to show up without calling, but I've come to a decision about the dude ranch." Her heels clicked across the polished hardwood.

The lawyer removed his reading glasses, peered at her. "And?"

"I don't want my share." She sank into the chair, set her purse in the floor at her feet.

"You're certain?"

"Yes. It should belong to the Donovan family. And I'm not one of them." Her eyes burned, but she blinked the tears away.

"Very well. If you're certain, I'll contact Chase and see if he'd like to buy you out. But we can't do anything officially, until your year is up."

"But he shouldn't have to purchase his family legacy. Isn't there any way I could sign my share over to him?"

"I'm afraid not." He stood, opened the top drawer of a file cabinet. "Eden's will is very clear. If you don't want your share, you have to sell it. You can't leave until September fifteenth. And you can't sell until July of next year."

"I don't understand why she even left me a share. I'm not family. She should have left it to her brother."

"She must have thought a lot of you—for her to leave half of her birthright to you." He pulled a file out, set it on his desk, reclaimed his chair and opened it. He set his glasses back on his nose as he scanned and flipped pages.

Landry felt like she was letting Eden down. But she couldn't stay. Not with Chase trying to snake his way into her heart just to get her share. And to think, she'd assumed he was so much like Eden. She would have never pulled anything like this.

And he'd thought Landry was a scam artist.

"It's not right for them to have to buy their family legacy from me. It's theirs and never should have been mine."

"There is one thing you might consider."

"What?"

"Eden's will states that if either party decides to sell their share, the seller sets the price." He looked up at her. "As long as the amount doesn't exceed fair market value."

Her distraught brain couldn't follow. "Meaning?"

"Meaning, you set the price as low as you'd like. No matter what the property is worth."

"So I could sell it for…a penny?"

"Yes. If you're certain that's what you want." Mr. Abbott closed the file, took his glasses off. "But I encourage you to think this through. You stand to lose a lot of money." He scribbled a figure on a piece of paper, pushed it across the desk for her to see. "This is what the dude ranch appraised for."

The zeroes boggled her mind. What had she been thinking? There was no way she could ever have bought Chase's share.

"Does this change anything?" Mr. Abbott asked.

"No." She looked up. "It's not about the money. It's about what's right. Can you draw the papers up for me?"

"As I said, you can't make the decision to sell until your year is up, but I can draw up a letter of intent to sell. I'll have them ready for you tomorrow. And come July fifteenth of next year, they won't be legally binding if you change your mind."

"I won't."

"You're a rare breed, Ms. Malone. Most people wouldn't walk away from this kind of money."

"Thank you for your time." She retrieved her purse and stood. "I'm leaving tomorrow, but I'd like to sign the papers before I go."

"First thing in the morning. But you still can't leave until September fifteenth."

"What have I got to lose by leaving early? What can Chase do, sue me? I'm giving him the property."

Mr. Abbott pursed his lips. "I wish more people lived by what's right instead of money. I'll contact Chase, let him know your decision."

"I'll tell him. Thank you for your help." She hurried out of the office.

Chase had told her back in the beginning that he'd do whatever it took to keep his legacy in his family. Somehow she'd never imagined he'd stoop so low.

Chase sat in the wingback in the foyer. Waiting up like a worried dad of a teenager. He didn't care if Landry figured him out. He wouldn't take the chance of missing her.

She'd stayed gone all day. A rendezvous with Kyle? But Kyle had claimed he wasn't interested. Maybe she'd driven home to visit her family.

The door opened and she stepped inside. She quickly spotted him, hesitated, then bolted for her quarters.

"We need to talk." He followed.

"I'm tired." Words tossed over her shoulder as she crossed the great room. She stopped only long enough to unlock her door, slip inside, slam it behind her.

Stiff, unyielding. Her body gave off stay-away vibes. But he couldn't just leave her alone. If this was about Kyle, he had to fight. To reveal his feelings. Stake his claim on her heart before it was too late. He couldn't just stand here and watch her hoping to waltz off into the sunset with another man. A man who claimed to be uninterested. A man unworthy of her.

And if it wasn't about Kyle, had Chase done something to upset her? Either way, he needed to see her. Talk to her. Find out what was wrong.

Decision made, he hurried to her door, rapped his knuckles three times.

"Who is it?" Her voice muffled.

"Chase. I told you, we need to talk."

"And I told you, I'm tired."

"It won't take long."

She opened the door, slipped out and shut it behind her. But not fast enough to block his view of the open suitcase on the wicker settee.

"Going somewhere?"

"Why do you care?" Her sharp words punched him in the gut.

"I do care, Landry. Where are you going?"

She wouldn't even look at him. Her eyes stayed riveted on his chest.

He cupped her cheek, gently raised her chin until she had no choice but to meet his eyes. Hers were glassy.

"What's wrong? Has something happened?"

"Stop acting like what I do matters to you." Bitterness steeled her gaze.

"You matter to me. What is wrong with you?"

"I'm not falling for it again. Leave me alone." She shoved his hand away, stepped back, opened her door and tried to slip inside.

But he got a foot in the threshold, stopping her from slamming the door in his face.

"Please, Chase," she begged on a sob. "Just leave me alone."

"I can't. Especially not when you're upset like this. Talk to me. Come down to the dock, where it's private."

"We don't have anything to talk about." She turned to face him.

"Maybe you don't. But I do. Have it your way." He bent, hauled her against him and slung her over his shoulder like a sack full of feed.

She sputtered, pummeled his back. "Put me down, you bully."

He stepped into the foyer.

"I didn't think you were going fishing until tomorrow." Mom wiped her hands on a dishcloth. "And that's not what I expected you to catch."

"We're just horsing around. Think I'll throw her in the pond."

"You'd better not." But Landry went silent. Probably embarrassed.

Mom shot him a knowing grin and opened the door for him.

His mom wouldn't normally approve of him

manhandling a woman. But she'd been trying to matchmake from the moment Landry arrived.

And now that he'd committed to it, he wouldn't rest until he settled things with Landry. Tonight.

Chapter Fifteen

As soon as they were out of earshot from the ranch house, Landry rained smacks over his back again. But he totally ignored her.

"Chase Donovan, if you don't put me down, I'll… I'll…" What? Cry. Hot tears ran up her forehead.

They made it to the dock, but surely he wouldn't toss her in.

"You wouldn't dare."

"Normally I might. But I brought you down here so we could talk, and tossing you in the river would only make you madder and more unreasonable."

"Put me down." Her voice broke. "Please."

He set her down. Ever so gently. As she tried to figure out a way to get around him and back to the house, he took one look at her tears and pulled her into his arms.

Right where she did but also didn't want to be.

All resistance went out of her. Maybe if she calmed down, she could catch him off guard. Make her escape. In the meantime, she let him hold her. How could he feel so good when none of it was real?

"Please don't cry." He cupped the back of her head in his big hand. "I didn't mean to upset you."

And she was making a blubbering idiot out of herself. *Pull it together. Don't let him know he hurt me.*

She sniffled, reined in the sobs, pulled out of his arms and swiped her face. Looking lovely— she could only imagine the damage to her makeup. And skin. She turned her back on him.

"What's wrong?"

Might as well be honest. Get it all out there. She didn't have anything else to lose. "I heard you."

"Heard me what?"

"I was in the barn last night. I heard your discussion with Nash."

He was quiet for a moment. "So you heard me tell Nash I'd been to see Kyle?" His tone regretful. "Please don't be angry."

"Kyle?"

"I guess you didn't hear everything?"

Only the part that cracked her heart in two. Why would he tell Nash where he'd been? "Why did you go to see him? Something about the hog hunt?"

"No. I told him to back off from you." His voice thick with emotion, he set his hands on her shoulders, turned her to face him. "But only because our little pretense became all too real for me."

"What?" Her gaze bounced up to meet his.

"I wanted Kyle to leave you alone so maybe you'd fall for me." His eyes were tender, promising forever.

Tears blurred her vision. But it wasn't real. She took a step back. She couldn't fall for his lie.

"I know you're still hung up on Kyle, and I won't pressure you." His hands fell to his sides. "The last thing I want is a rebound relationship. I'm willing to be your friend and business partner and that's all. If you're comfortable with that."

"But I'm not comfortable with that." Her voice wobbled. "Because I don't believe you. The visiting Kyle thing was a brilliant move on your part. But you see, I heard Nash say you were playing me."

"Oh. That." He massaged the back of his neck, then looked up at the sky. "Nash wouldn't know love if it bit him in the backside. He made an ugly assumption. Tried to call me on it. So I told him where I'd been, fired him in return."

"To keep him quiet."

"For disrespect. Toward me. And you. Along with paying way too much attention to our female staff and guests. It's been coming for a while." He caught her gaze again. "All I want is a chance with you."

"But you don't want me. You only want the ranch." She shook her head. "It's so clear now. I can't believe I fell for your act."

"It's not an act. I love you."

"Don't say that to me!" She hugged herself. "You're only pretending to love me so you can get my share of the dude ranch."

"You can't take the words of a bitter, miserable man for truth. Besides, it doesn't even make sense. Listen to yourself, Landry. You can't sign the dude ranch over to me. You have to sell it. And you can't do that until your year is up. Pretending to love you wouldn't benefit me at all." He took a step closer to her. "But loving you would. If I can convince you to love me back."

"Just stop." She held her hands up like a shield. Her laugh came out sarcastic. "I'm not stupid. If you married me, you wouldn't have to worry about buying my share of the dude ranch. And you thought I was the con artist. Or was that part of the act, too?"

"There's no act." His shoulders slumped. "I don't know how to convince you."

"Don't bother. You won." She took another step back and her heel slid off the dock. Teetering, she grabbed at air.

Chase steadied her, then backed away. "Please come this way. I won't touch you again. Just be careful."

"I went to see your lawyer this afternoon." She took two steps toward him, her heart still in her throat. "He's drawing up a letter of my intent to sell, and they'll be ready in the morning. You can have your precious ranch for a penny come next July."

He held his hands up in surrender. "That's not what I want."

"I'm going in to sign the papers first thing, and then I'm going home. To people I can trust."

"You can trust me. All I want is to love you, Landry. If you can't love me back, I can live with that. Just stay here and help me run this place. You're so good at all the stuff that bores me to tears. I need you here."

"Save it. And move out of my way. If you try manhandling me again, I won't be embarrassed this time. I'll scream bloody murder until all the guests hear. Which wouldn't be good for your precious business."

He hesitated, then stepped aside, clearing her path.

She ran all the way to the ranch house. At least the foyer was empty, the great room abandoned as she darted through. She didn't stop until she'd locked herself in Granny's private quarters. She should have finished packing. Instead, she lay across Granny's bed. And sobbed.

The next morning, as soon as William Abbott pulled up outside his office, Chase got out of his truck.

"Mr. Donovan." William tipped his cowboy hat. "What can I do for you this fine morning?"

"I don't want to buy the ranch from Miss Malone."

William's mouth opened, shut, opened again. "I'm not at liberty to discuss the situation without Miss Malone present."

"Come on, William. You're my family lawyer."

Her white Chevy Malibu slowed, turned in to the lot. He saw Landry's jaw drop when she spotted him. She sat in her car, looking as if she wasn't getting out.

He strolled over, tried to open her door but found it locked.

"Come on, Landry." He splayed his hands. "You can't stay in there all day."

The mechanism clicked. He opened her door for her.

"What are you doing here?" She ignored the hand he offered her.

An idea took shape. "I came to sign the papers."

"But I thought—" William's mouth clamped shut. He scurried for his office.

Thank goodness the man hadn't blown it.

Landry's lips tightened, but at least she got out of the car.

The lawyer held the door open for her and Chase followed her in, nodding to the secretary.

"Susan, hold my calls, will you?" William asked.

"Of course, sir."

Landry settled in the chair across from the desk, Chase beside her.

William pulled the file from his cabinet, opened it, read the legalese, made sure they both understood. Then pushed the document toward Landry.

"This is only a letter of intent. On July fifteenth of next year, if Miss Malone hasn't changed her mind, I'll draw up legally binding papers for the sale. Upon both of your signatures and once the penny changes hands, Chase will need to file them with the county clerk.

"Miss Malone will continue to run her share of the ranch until September fifteenth, at which time she'll appoint a manager in her stead."

Landry's jaw dropped. "But I told you, I'm leaving. Today."

"And as I tried to explain yesterday, according to Eden's will—" William's tone remained steady, persuasive "—you and Chase have to fulfill the two months of running the dude ranch together before any decisions can be made. A decision to sell can't be made until the year has passed. You can sign the papers today, but nothing will be legally binding until—"

"I'll sign it." Landry picked up the pen, signed on the appropriate line, slid it over to Chase. "But I'm leaving. Today."

His hand grazed hers, and a lightning bolt shot up his arm. He picked up the letter, ripped it in two.

"What are you doing?" Landry's gaze met his. He tore the document again just for good measure. "Could we use your conference room, William?"

"Of course." The lawyer grinned. He stood, led them down a hall to the right, opened a door, ushered them inside.

The door shut behind William. And Chase turned to face the love of his life.

"Why did you do that?" Legs too unsteady to hold her up any longer, Landry sank into the nearest chair at the long table.

"Because I'm not interested in buying your half of the dude ranch."

"But this is what you've wanted. From the beginning."

"It's not what I want anymore." He turned her chair to face him, knelt in front of her. "I want you. I want us to run the ranch together."

"Why are you doing this?" She closed her eyes, wanting to believe him. Afraid to.

"Because I love you. I want to marry you and live happily ever after."

Just as convincing as he'd been on the dock last night. Only now he'd proven he wasn't after her share of the ranch. He'd had his chance and torn up the papers.

Something raw tore through her. "I can't do this. I trusted my feelings once. Trusted a man once, and look where that got me."

"But I'm not Kyle. I won't leave you. Ever."

Words she longed to hear. Longed to believe.

"What are you afraid of?" he asked.

"Everything." Tears burned, then fell from her eyes.

"Tell me." He stood, pulled her to her feet.

"I thought I loved Kyle. But I didn't. I thought he loved me, but he didn't."

"I don't know how to convince you. Maybe it'll just take time." He traced a tear with his thumb, stirring the rhythm of her heart. "We can go back to being friends, then maybe build on it. But if you never think of me as any more than a friend, I'm okay with that. As long as you're in my life. Please stay, Landry. Stay and help me run the ranch."

And again, she saw it—a glimpse of forever in his eyes.

"But running the dude ranch was never your dream," she said.

"You're my dream. I want to handle all the entertainment stuff while you take care of the business part. I want what my parents have—both of us utilizing our talents to make a great team."

"Then why did you stay away all those years? I thought you wanted to travel."

"It's not that I wanted to travel so much as I didn't want any regrets. I didn't want to look back someday and wish I'd traveled like Gramps did. But once I was on the road, I missed this place. It's home." He cupped her face in his hands. "Especially with you there. Stay with me."

She took a wobbly breath—as all arguments and

questions emptied from her heart. "I'll stay. But the friend part. I don't think it will work."

His mouth straight lined.

"It won't work because I love you, too."

He closed his eyes. "You have no idea how much I want to believe that." His hand dropped away from her face. "But give yourself time to heal, and when you're ready—if you ever get ready—I'll be here."

Heart swelling, she leaned into his shoulder. Soaked up his warmth, his love. How could she convince him her feelings were as real as his?

"You know," she said, "when we ran into Kyle, it stirred everything up. But it also helped me understand something. I didn't realize it at the time, but he tried to change me into what he wanted. I never wanted to own a bed-and-breakfast. I wanted a dude ranch. And he had me wearing dresses and business suits. It's a wonder he didn't ask me to bleach my hair blond."

She pulled back enough to trace Chase's jaw with her fingertips. "I wanted to fall in love, to make my happily-ever-after come true, so I tried to make it happen. And I thought I had. But I never loved Kyle."

"If you never loved him, why did I catch your tears over him?"

"It wasn't about him. It was about me. When I saw him again—I realized I'd almost married a man I didn't love. I cried because I was confused. I'd finally met the man of my dreams, but I couldn't trust myself to pursue anything with you."

"But you trust your heart now? How do you know you really love me?" His voice cracked, obviously needing, craving her assurance, like she'd craved his.

"I never missed Kyle. He traveled a lot for his business and I'd go for months at a time without seeing him, but I never missed him." She gazed into Chase's eyes—hoping he could see inside her heart. "You were gone for one day, and I thought I'd go insane with missing you."

A cocky smile tugged at his handsome lips.

"I never knew real love," she said. "Not until you kissed me and I couldn't breathe or think. Everything inside me imploded, and I realized the only one I've ever loved is you. The only one I'd like to spend the rest of my days with is—"

His lips grazed hers, cutting off her words, soft and sweet. So tender her heart soared, her brain stalled and her breathing stilled.

This was real.

But he soon pulled away.

"The only one I'd rather spend time with instead of going fishing is you," he whispered. "The only one who keeps me from thinking straight—"

"—is you." Her voice blended with his.

"But I don't want to be your business partner anymore."

"Why not?" Her brain was way too foggy to keep up.

"I want to be your husband. We can take things slow. But in the end, I plan to be your husband."

"Oh." Her breath hitched. "I think that can be arranged." She quirked an eyebrow. "But you might need to kiss me again. Just to convince me." She closed her eyes, tipped her head back.

"My pleasure." His lips met hers.

And turned her to mush.

Chase ended the kiss, looked deep in her eyes. "I have something for you."

The corners of her mouth kicked up. "I don't think I need anything else."

He grinned, pulled a small black box from his pocket.

Heart revving, her gaze went to the box, met his, then moved back to the box. "I thought we said slow."

"It's not—this isn't." He opened the box.

Granny's cameo. "Oh." A mixture of relief and disappointment whooshed out with the tiny word.

"She left it to Eden. It's costume, not worth anything."

"But worth gold because your grandfather gave it to her."

"Eden left it to me. To give to my wife someday. Until then, I'd like to be your man. The only one to fasten your necklaces." He stepped behind her. "Hold your hair up."

"The best offer of my life." A shudder went through her as he fastened the clasp. His hands moved away, and the cameo fell heavy at the hollow of her collarbone.

"The only one you kiss," he said.

She pressed a hand to the cameo. "I like that idea. A lot."

"Let's go home." He turned her to face him, brushed his lips across hers.

Set her heart into orbit. "If I can still walk."

He winked at her. Then, hand in hand, they strolled down the hall to Mr. Abbott's office.

The lawyer looked up. "Have you come to an agreement?"

"We're going to run the dude ranch together." Chase squeezed her hand. "With a wedding in our future."

"Well, in that case—" Mr. Abbott grinned "—I have something for you." He ambled to his file cabinet, pulled out an envelope. "I'll leave you alone while you read it."

Chase took the letter bearing his and Landry's names on it in familiar swirled cursive.

Landry gasped. "That's Eden's handwriting."

"Yes."

Landry leaned against his side as he pulled a letter out, then started reading aloud.

Dear Chase and Landry,
If you're reading this, my devious plan worked. I wish I could be there to witness it.

Y'all are the most stubborn people I know. For years, I tried to get you to date each other. I knew you'd make the perfect match, but neither of you would work with me. I can't believe it took my death to make it happen.

Love each other, trust each other, rely on each other. Give Mom and Dad grandchildren someday. Be happy. And say it out loud, together—Eden was so right.

Landry's vision hopelessly blurred. Chase's hand shook as he refolded the letter, then looked down at her.

"Eden was *so* right." Their voices blended.

And forever settled in her rapidly beating heart. He was hers. And she was his.

Epilogue

"You ready?" Landry's dad asked as he kissed her cheek.

"So ready." She giggled, then clamped a hand over her mouth. She stood at the top of the landing while guests and her groom waited downstairs. Wearing a traditional dress she'd picked with her mother and sister.

"You really love him."

"I do." Her hands didn't even tremble as she clutched her keepsake silk bouquet of trailing wisteria mixed with white and turquoise lilies.

"I can tell this time." Daddy offered his arm. "And more importantly—to me, anyway—he loves you."

The wedding march started, and her father slowly escorted her down the stairs. They paused in the foyer. The lattice arch draped with lavender wisteria, candelabras flanking the fireplace, and yards of tulle with turquoise ribbon transformed the great room into a wedding chapel.

Half of Aubrey had made the trip for the wedding. Former coworkers, family and friends. Along with their new Bandera friends. Devree was her maid of honor. Ally and her former boss, Rayna, pulled bridesmaid duty along with her new/old friend Resa.

But the most important person there was her groom. Surrounded by more girly decorations than any of the weddings they'd booked. Yet Chase didn't seem to mind at all as he waited for her by the fireplace, right where he was supposed to be.

Daddy escorted her slowly down the aisle.

Finally she stood by Chase's side. His eyes reflected the color of the turquoise cummerbund he hadn't even raised a fuss about. The devotion in their depths along with his sappy smile testified she was the only one for him.

"Who gives this woman to be married in holy matrimony?" their pastor asked.

Daddy cleared his throat. "Her mother and I." He kissed her cheek again, then eased her hand from his arm, linked her fingers with Chase's.

"Let's get this knot tied, preacher." Chase shot her a wink.

A wave a chuckles spread through the crowd.

The vows they repeated were simple, timeless, life-bonding, sealing the love she'd longed for. The kind of love she'd found with Chase.

"I now pronounce you husband and wife. Chase, you may kiss your bride."

"You're all mine now," he whispered as his arms encircled her waist and their gazes met. "I'm not going anywhere. Ever. And there's no pretending about it."

Tears slipped from beneath her lashes as his kiss confirmed his promise of forever.

No more winning over the cowboy. And no more pretending. This was real. For both of them.

* * * * *

If you loved Chase and Landry's story, be sure to pick up the first in the TEXAS COWBOYS *series:*

REUNITING WITH THE COWBOY

You may also enjoy these emotionally gripping and wonderful stories:

THE RANCHER'S TEXAS MATCH
by Brenda Minton
A FAMILY FOR THE FARMER
by Laurel Blount
SECOND CHANCE ROMANCE
by Jill Weatherholt

Available now from Love Inspired!

Find more great reads at www.LoveInspired.com

Dear Reader,

Headlines and movies sometimes leave me pondering. My recent musings? How could people dump fiancés they supposedly love at the altar? Why wait until the ceremony to end things through public humiliation? And how does the dumpee move on? I explored these questions through Landry and Chase.

When Landry arrived in Bandera, Texas, two very different people were thrown together by an inheritance. In fact, the only thing Chase and Landry had in common was a love for his deceased sister. On top of that, Chase didn't trust Landry and thought she scammed her way into the dude ranch. But determined not to return to her entire hometown's pity, she resolved to win him over.

Chase tested Landry's staying power and she passed with flying colors, much to his chagrin. Things began to change as they worked together to ensure the dude ranch's future and Chase got a glimpse of her shattered heart. As he softened toward her, they bonded over their mutual loss. But as their feelings developed, Landry had to allow God to help her overcome bitterness, and Chase had to surrender his trust issues before they could build a future together.

I always miss my characters when I finish a

book, but I enjoy getting a glimpse of them in future tales. This series will continue with Resa, so watch for her story soon.

Blessings,
Shannon Taylor Vannatter

Get 2 Free Books,
Plus 2 Free Gifts—
just for trying the Reader Service!

LIS17R

Get 2 Free Books,
Plus 2 Free Gifts—
just for trying the
Reader Service!

HOMETOWN HEARTS ♡

YES! Please send me **The Hometown Hearts Collection** in Larger Print. This collection begins with 3 FREE books and 2 FREE gifts in the first shipment. Along with my 3 free books, I'll also get the next 4 books from the Hometown Hearts Collection, in LARGER PRINT, which I may either return and owe nothing, or keep for the low price of $4.99 U.S./ $5.89 CDN each plus $2.99 for shipping and handling per shipment*. If I decide to continue, about once a month for 8 months I will get 6 or 7 more books, but will only need to pay for 4. That means 2 or 3 books in every shipment will be FREE! If I decide to keep the entire collection, I'll have paid for only 32 books because 19 books are FREE! I understand that accepting the 3 free books and gifts places me under no obligation to buy anything. I can always return a shipment and cancel at any time. My free books and gifts are mine to keep no matter what I decide.

262 HCN 3432 462 HCN 3432

Name	(PLEASE PRINT)	
Address		Apt. #
City	State/Prov.	Zip/Postal Code

Signature (if under 18, a parent or guardian must sign)

Mail to the **Reader Service**:
IN U.S.A.: P.O. Box 1867, Buffalo, NY. 14240-1867
IN CANADA: P.O. Box 609, Fort Erie, Ontario L2A 5X3

* Terms and prices subject to change without notice. Prices do not include applicable taxes. Sales tax applicable in NY. Canadian residents will be charged applicable taxes. This offer is limited to one order per household. All orders subject to approval. Credit or debit balances in a customer's account(s) may be offset by any other outstanding balance owed by or to the customer. Please allow 4 to 6 weeks for delivery. Offer available while quantities last. Offer not available to Quebec residents.

> **Your Privacy**—The Reader Service is committed to protecting your privacy. Our Privacy Policy is available online at www.ReaderService.com or upon request from the Reader Service.
>
> We make a portion of our mailing list available to reputable third parties that offer products we believe may interest you. If you prefer that we not exchange your name with third parties, or if you wish to clarify or modify your communication preferences, please visit us at www.ReaderService.com/consumerschoice or write to us at Reader Service Preference Service, P.O. Box 9062, Buffalo, NY. 14240-9062. Include your complete name and address.